The Lottery

A novel adapted from the original screenplay

By

Roman Gutierrez

This work is protected under copyright laws and is the intellectual property of Roman Gutierrez. All rights reserved. No part of this work may be reproduced, distributed, or transmitted in any form or by any means, including photocopying, recording, or other electronic or mechanical methods, without the prior written permission of the copyright owner, except in the case of brief quotations embodied in critical reviews and certain other noncommercial uses permitted by copyright law.

For permission requests, please contact:

www.Good-Books.org

The copyright owner asserts their moral rights to the work, including the right to be identified as the author and the right to the integrity of the work.

Any unauthorized use of this work, including but not limited to reproduction, distribution, modification, or public display, may result in civil and criminal penalties under applicable copyright laws.

If you have any questions or concerns regarding the copyright, use or distribution of this work or original screenplay, The Lottery ©. Please contact Roman Gutierrez at Good-Books.org for clarification.

By accessing or using this work, you agree to be bound by the terms and conditions of this copyright disclaimer.

© 2024 Roman Gutierrez. All rights reserved.

ISBN: 979-8-9905871-0-6

Dedicated to my wife who inspires me.

Also dedicated to my mother, who put up with me.

~Prologue~

War exacts a heavy toll on the men and women who fight in it, leaving them with deep physical and emotional scars that can last a lifetime. Beyond the obvious dangers of injury or death on the battlefield, soldiers often face less visible but equally devastating forms of collateral damage. The horrors of combat can lead to post-traumatic stress disorder (PTSD), a debilitating condition characterized by anxiety, depression, flashbacks, and nightmares.

Many veterans struggle to reintegrate into civilian life, feeling disconnected from loved ones and society at large. Substance abuse, domestic violence, and suicide rates are alarmingly high among former service members as they grapple with the psychological aftermath of war. Even those who escape direct physical harm may carry the weight of survivor's guilt, haunted by the memory of fallen comrades. The true cost of war for the men and women who fight in it is immeasurable, extending far beyond the battlefield and impacting their lives and the lives of those around them for years to come.

Jack Peterson is like many who return from war and hopefully this story will assist the reader in understanding those who struggle with PTSD; most of whom do so in silence.

Contents

<u>Chapter One</u>

~ Sweetwater ~

At the Riddell Ranch on the outskirts of the small town of Sweetwater Texas, the evening is peaceful. Bulls and cows grazed gently in the pasture while the old windmill turned lazily. The red and orange sky appeared to swallow the earth, washing it in a celestial glow. From outside the ranch house, you could see the activity of the family finishing their evening dinner in the kitchen.

Inside the cozy front room, Henry Riddell sat nervously on the couch.

A rugged cowboy in his late 50s, Henry was the stereotypical hardworking Texas rancher. Dressed in blue jeans and a cowboy shirt, his thick accent signaling his birthplace.

In the kitchen, his wife Bell is cleaning up from their evening meal. Though petite, Bell looked like she could handle her fair share of ranch work. The eclectic decor mixed old west style with more modern touches. The ancient Curtis Mathis console TV set is still working, thanks to hardly ever being used.

Henry leaned forward anxiously; his gaze fixed on the flickering television screen. From the kitchen, Bell catches a glimpse of Henry nervously on the couch leaned in towards the TV and she calls out, "Honey, don't be so nervous. You're getting yourself all worked up."

"I can't help myself darlin", Henry replied, wringing his hands. "I don't know if I can watch..."

Bell sensing Henry's discomfort. "Sweetie, do you want to turn it off? We can just check the numbers later…"

The lotto announcer's voice suddenly broke the silence. "And now everybody sit back and get ready for your lucky lotto numbers."

"Here we go, Darlin", Henry exclaimed.

The announcer began reading off the numbers. "And your first lucky number is 23."

"That's right, I've got 23", Henry said eagerly.

Bell made her way in from the kitchen wiping her hands on a dishtowel. She takes a seat beside her husband. "What...you've got the first number?"

"Hold it down, honey..." Henry cautioned.

With each subsequent number called, Henry and Bell grew more excited and anxious. By the time the sixth and final number was announced, they could hardly believe their luck.

"31, and that's your last lotto number tonight for 35 million dollars. Good luck everyone and good night!" the announcer concluded.

Henry jumped up and down, overjoyed. "I told you that son of a gun was tellin' the truth! All our prayers have been answered!"

Bell flopped back against the couch cushions in disbelief. "35 million dollars...My God Henry, that's so much money."

"More like 17 million since we get it all at once," Henry said breathlessly. "But what the hell? That's more than enough money, darlin'!"

Tears streamed down Bell's face as the shock set in. "Is this a dream, Henry? We don't have to leave?"

Henry embraced her tightly. "You're damn right we don't. Your damn right..."

In the days and weeks that followed, the lucky Riddell's' lives were transformed. But for Henry and Bell, their windfall meant only one thing; saving the Riddell ranch.

Six weeks after their unbelievable stroke of luck, Henry is keeping an appointment at Connie's Cafe in downtown Sweetwater. As Henry pulls up in his old pickup truck, he spotted a sharply dressed Englishman already seated inside. John Smith, about 60 years old and impeccably groomed in a suit and tie, looked painfully out of place in the rustic Texas eatery.

Henry walked in and made his way to John's booth, greeting him warmly. "Mr. Smith?"

The distinguished man slowly raised his head and tips his hat. "Good day to you Mr. Riddell, how are you this fine afternoon?"

"Fine sir, and yourself?" Henry replied.

"I am feeling very well today, thank you for asking." John glanced at his watch.

Henry checked his own timepiece anxiously. "I was sure you said 11 o'clock."

"I did indeed, sir," John assured him, "and by my watch, you are early. Please, sit down."

As Henry slid into the booth, he spoke earnestly. "Mr. Smith, I can't tell you how much I am in debt to you. The fact is you probably saved my life."

John acknowledged the praise modestly. "I assure you that the pleasure indeed was all mine."

"Maybe you don't really understand what I mean," Henry insisted. "I was going to lose everything in just two days. Everything that I had ever worked for, that farm...That patch of dirt had been in my family since before Texas was even a state. From my great great grandaddy on down they are all buried on that property." He hung his head, getting choked up. "It was just too much to bear. I was losing something that was passed down for generations and it was ending with me. That's why I say you saved my life. You saved that farm, with over a hundred and fifty years of blood and sweat from my family. I can never repay the debt of gratitude I owe you."

John reached across the table and patted Henry's calloused hand. "I do appreciate your gratitude. I am very thankful that I could be of service to you and your family. It is always a pleasure to know that one's deeds are appreciated. In your particular case, it warms my heart to know that something very special was preserved."

With tears welling in his eyes, Henry slid an envelope across the table to the Englishman. "I just wanted you to know how much this means..."

"I assure you Henry, the pleasure indeed was all mine."

Henry cleared his throat. "The check is made out just like you asked, and I even added a little extra if that's okay?"

With a pleased smile, "That was very generous of you," Mr. Smith replied graciously.

"No sir, that isn't quite enough as far as I'm concerned."

"Henry, you've done your part and I... well I have done mine."

After a moment's hesitation, Henry asked, "Can I ask you a question?"

"Surely, go right ahead."

Nervously trying to find the words, "Well, I just...um, how exactly…" Henry continues to struggle.

Mr. Smith saved him the trouble. "How did I do it, is that right?"

Wide eyed Henry nodded. "Yes sir."

"Well, I've never really understood it completely, but I can tell you it's still quite amazing to even to myself."

Henry looked a bit sheepish. "So, you can see the future?"

Mr. Smith chuckled. "Not as much as I would like, or I wouldn't have any speeding tickets now, would I?" He winked conspiratorially. "But for the purposes of this conversation...Let's just say I have a tremendous insight in at least one area."

Henry let out a slight laugh of relief. "Yes sir, you surely do."

The two men shook hands firmly before stepping outside the cafe. "Well, it was indeed a pleasure and I wish you only the best in the future, Mr. Riddell," Mr. Smith said.

"The same to you," Henry replied. "I hope I'll hear from you soon."

"I'll try and stay in touch."

"Anything you want...Don't hesitate."

As John Smith walked towards his sports car, he turned back and called out, "Henry, you take care of that farm now!"

"Yes sir, I'll do that," Henry promised, watching the enigmatic man drive away.

Eight months later, San Diego, California.

Joe's Place was a little hole in the wall bar located on a not too busy street. Though small, it had a cozy atmosphere. On the jukebox, a 60s tune played, matching the dated decor. The patrons were mostly men enjoying beers and telling tales; it was clearly a cop hangout.

The local newscast is blaring up on the TV. "Remember all that Y2K doom and gloom? Three months later and it all seemed to be way overblown. Debora is downtown talking to local businesses..."

Tony, the bartender, turns down the TV with the remote.

At one end of the bar sat Jack Peterson, nursing a rum and coke in contemplative silence, Jack is in his early 50's and nearly at his limit judging by how he fumbled with the glass. The bartender, Tony, caught sight of him. "Jack...Jack, come on, you've had enough."

Jack was unresponsive at first, until Tony repeated his name more firmly. "Jack!"

"What? Oh Tony, you worry too much. I was just thinking."

"Yeah, and I was just thinking you're done," Tony quipped, picking up the empty glass and putting it in the sink. "Not tonight, let me get you a ride, Jackie."

"You're no fun," Jack protested. "Come on...one more for the road?"

He sits a few moments in silence, then Jack asked philosophically, "Say, you ever wonder just what the hell we're doing here?",

Tony gave him a look. "You see...now I know you're done." Tony laughs, he's heard this line of questioning numerous times while slopping drinks.

"No, I'm serious," Jack insisted. "I mean, what do we do it all for? You work for 40 plus years. You buy crap you don't need and then...poof! It's all gone..."

There is a noticeable silence for a few moments

Tony quips, "Look, if you're talking about the meaning of life, I've heard more than a few explanations slopping drinks for the past 25 years. But none of them summed it up better than this: It all means more a few minutes before it's over."

Jack raised his glass ironically. "Same goes for 'last call' I suppose."

Tony laughed and then regarded Jack more seriously for a few beats. "Seriously though Jackie, is everything alright?"

Jack remained silent while staring at the empty glass, "Yeah, I guess. I had a bad dream."

Tony looks at Jack concerned, "A bad dream, huh?"

"Yep, back in country."

Recognizing the reference, Tony nodded slowly.

The bartender could relate. "Man, I hate those...I haven't had one in years, but brother, I know how it feels."

Jack explained, "It was like I was there again, even the smells. All scared and jacked up at the same time." He paused, then added, "Like how you feel getting on a rollercoaster, only this rollercoaster occasionally goes right off the tracks."

"Hey, that's a great way to put it," Tony admitted, "I wasn't stationed on the front line, but I saw enough action to know I didn't want more."

As Jack stared down at the bar, Tony poured him another drink and knocked on the worn wood of the bar to get his attention. "This one's on the house."

"Thanks," Jack mumbled.

"I was stationed in Saigon. Where were you at?" Tony asked.

Jack hesitated a long beat before answering. "Khe Sanh in 68."

Tony let out a huff. "Jesus, I didn't know you were there."

With a haunted look, Jack replied, "Hell...I guess I tried to forget all about it. I buried it along with all those Marines."

"That was a hell of a battle," Tony said somberly. "I seem to remember that being a real meat grinder."

Jack nodded, the memories coming back vividly. "What I remembered most was the noise." Jack paused a long moment

"It all started in late January in 68, Charlie hit the ammunition dump right off. A direct freakin' hit. Ninety percent of the ordinance was in there, but it didn't go up all at once. Those mortars were still going off a day later. When we needed supplies or evac the air support would drop those 2000 pound bombs in the tree line it would literally lift you right off your feet." His voice grew distant. "Noise, that's what kept you alert...the damn noise."

"I remember that being a long one", the bartender said.

Jack took a sip of his drink before answering flatly. "77 days." He paused, the memories weighing heavily on him. "155 Marines killed".

Tony waited for Jack to continue, sensing the pain.

"Hell, I figured I'd get drafted in the lottery anyway, so I enlisted with a buddy."

Jack stared at the amber liquid in his glass, seeing another time and place. "Jim and I just two dumb kids from San Diego. We didn't know our ass from a hole in the ground. That's why they draft 18 year old's; they don't know any better.

He paused again; the recollection clearly difficult.

Jack fell silent for a long moment, the distant echo of explosions replaying in his mind. "Seventy-seven damn days." A sad smile tugged at his lips.

Tony wipes off another shot glass, He peeks up at Jack. "That was the dream?"

Jack nodded. "Yep." He was quiet for a bit, then admitted, "Not sure why it's still rattling around in my head 32 years later. But here we are." Jack tries to laugh it off.

The bartender gets serious and leans in. "Jackie, seriously, you should talk to someone. Holding it all inside ain't good."

"Wait, I thought I just did?" Jack gives off a laugh."

"Come on, you know what I mean."

The two men sat in silence for a long moment before Jack drained the last of his drink and fumbled for his keys. "Ah...I best get going."

"Jack, come on..." Tony eyed him skeptically. "How about a ride? You can get your car in the morning."

Jack waved him off. "Come on, I live four blocks away...I'll be alright."

But Tony was insistent. "Let me get you a ride." He motioned to a couple of cops nursing coffees at the other end of the bar, who nodded and rose from their stools.

Realizing he was outnumbered; Jack responds to all of them. "I'm fine. Don't worry, have a good night, boys, Tony."

He composed himself and headed for the door as Tony gave the cops a meaningful look. Outside, Jack fumbled with his keys trying to get them in the ignition of his car.

Moments later, a patrol car pulled up behind Jack's car, light bar flashing as the spotlight illuminated Jack's vehicle. They pullup alongside him.

"Hey Jack, how's it going?" the cop in the passenger seat called out jovially.

Jack sighed. "Great, you boys busy?"

"Yeah, kind of, we have to follow a guy home from the bar." Both cops' smile.

Muttering a curse at Tony under his breath, Jack asked resignedly, "I guess I don't have a choice, right?"

"No," the cop confirmed with a sympathetic wink. "But hey, it could be worse. You could be sitting in the back."

Minutes later, Jack pulled up in front of his apartment building, tires bumping the curb. The patrol car pulls alongside of him again as he got out.

"Have a good one, Jack," the cop called out.

"Thanks, catch some bad guys for me."

As Jack made his way inside, the two cops had a quiet conversation in their vehicle. "He sure tied one on for a Sunday," the passenger remarked.

The driver nodded. "Jack was a hell of a cop. It must be tough for him to be on the outside now."

"Early retirement, I wish they'd make me take one."

"Guys like that don't have anything else," the driver said somberly. "For them it's a life sentence."

Inside his ground floor sparse apartment, Jack turned on the TV and raised the volume, then poured himself another drink in the kitchen. He settled onto the couch, staring sightlessly at the television and sipping slowly, fighting the onset of sleep and drunkenness. The clock read 12:35 AM when he finally passed out.

The next morning, Jack awoke in a daze to the sound of the TV blaring. He was sprawled out on the couch, still fully dressed from the night before. Rubbing his eyes groggily, he glanced at the wall clock 7:41 AM. "Damnit." He rose unsteadily and shuffled to the bathroom, splashing water on his face. Staring at his reflection, he traced the lines etched into his face as if seeing them for the first time, the physical reminders of sleepless nights and day after relentless day on the force.

It was almost as if Jack had awoken as a different, older man than when he first dozed off.

Later that morning, soft blues music played from a brick building in downtown San Diego. The sign on the door reads "Peterson Investigations." Jack sat in his small private office, feet up on the desk as he studied old photographs and memorabilia from his lengthy career. There was his retirement plaque from the SDPD after 26 years of service, citations and commendations for outstanding police work, his P.I. license, and faded snapshots that marked the different stages of his life.

In one, a youthful and cocky Jack stood beside his friend Jimmy in their Marine uniforms, a lifetime ago. Another showed him with his wife and young son, back when his future seemed bright, and the possibilities were endless. Now a widower and his son grown, Jack is alone with only memories and regrets for company. Sipping from a glass, Jack stared wistfully at the photos and mementos, replaying his life's journey. The cluttered office was a physical manifestation of his mind, out of order and in dire need of being straightened up. But where would he even start?

The shrill ringing of the telephone broke through Jack's reverie. He picked up the receiver. "Peterson Investigations, can I help you?"

"Jack, how the hell are you?" came a familiar voice on the other end.

It was Ben Klein; an attorney Jack had worked with frequently over the years.

"Ben, what the heck have you been up to? Nice to hear from you."

"It's been a while," Ben agreed.

"The Walker case about six months ago, right?" Jack recalled.

"Yeah, that's right. You made out pretty good on that one."

Jack smirked. "I need a few more like that."

"Well, I think I've got one right up your alley," Ben said with a hint of mystery.

"Another divorce?" Jack assumed.

"No, this one is pretty interesting."

Jack's ears perk up, "Now you've got me all curious."

"It's kind of complicated so why don't we meet..." Ben paused. "How about some lunch today?"

Jack thumbed through his empty day planner just for show. "I guess I could push a couple things around."

"Fine, how's 2 o'clock at Di Puccio's?"

"That place over on Thompson?" Jack verified.

"That's it."

"Well two it is then."

"See you there."

After hanging up, Jack leaned back in his chair, his gaze returning to the framed photos and memorabilia surrounding his desk.

The memories came flooding back unbidden...

It was over six years into his marriage with Margaret. She was a stunning woman in her late 20s, who didn't rely on her beauty to get by. This particular night, an innocent question had quickly escalated into a heated argument in their kitchen while young Shawn tried not to eavesdrop from the living room.

"I'm going to take care of it damn it, don't worry," Jack insisted angrily.

"Again? One more time you're going to take care of it?" Margaret shot back, her voice rising. "How many more times are you going to put us in the hole? When does it end?"

She snatched up some overdue bills from the counter. "These, what are we going to do about

these? We have no money...You're sick, Jack. You
need help!

"Jesus Christ, Margaret, not the damn
speech again about how Jack drinks and gambles
too much!" he spat. "You remember I put the food
on the table, I keep a roof over our heads. You
never go without...I find a way."

But Margaret was insistent. "For how long,
Jack? How long? We've been lucky for all these
years. You've got to think about your son."

"I don't think about him?" Jack was
incredulous. "I don't go out and put my ass on the
line, in the street every day for the both of you?"

"You put your ass on the line for your
goddamn self," Margaret retorted bitterly. "If you
didn't do that every day, Jack would cease to exist."

Outraged, Jack fired back, "Oh, I see...I do it
for fun, right? I like risking my freaking life for
nothing. You're not on the job every day, so you
don't understand."

"And everything I do for you and this
family, that means nothing?" Margaret's voice
shook with anger and hurt. "Because I don't get a
paycheck? Because I'm not hooked on adrenaline
like you? I'd rather work than put up with your

condescending attitude. I thought I stayed home for all of us?"

With chilling finality, Jack declared, "You see, you're just being ungrateful."

"I should be grateful that you come stumbling in at all hours, broke?" Margaret cried. "Oh, of course you hit the big one a couple times a year, but it never makes up for all the losses. You could win every day for a month and not make up for it."

Fed up, Jack turned to storm out. "I'm not going to listen to this crap, it just never ends with you...does it?"

"It will end, Jack," Margaret said, her voice trembling with unshed tears. "Maybe sooner than you think."

Jack wheeled around, outraged at what he perceived as a threat. "Don't threaten me, Margaret!"

But Margaret just looked at him sadly through her tears. "The sad thing is, Jack, it's not a threat...and you don't even know it."

The haunting memory faded as Jack became aware of his surroundings once more. Shaking off the past.

<u>Chapter Two</u>

~ The Job ~

Jack grabs his jacket and headed out to meet Ben Klein for their 2 o'clock lunch appointment.

The Italian restaurant was fairly empty when Jack arrived. Ben looked every bit the young, polished professional in his suit and briefcase. Jack had made an effort to smarten up as well, wearing slacks and a sport coat over his slightly rumpled shirt.

After some idle small talk over their meals, Ben reached into his briefcase and pulled out a folder. "Well, this is why I thought we should meet. I've got this client, Kathy Burns, who's going through probate and she is concerned about a few investments her mother made before she died."

Jack flashed a knowing grin. "How many millions are missing?"

When Ben responded matter of factly, "Just 12,"

Jack nearly choked on his food. "12 million, Jesus I was just kidding."

"Yeah, 12 million bucks," Ben confirmed with a smirk, "and she seems very determined to get to the bottom of it."

Regaining his composure, Jack asked, "What kind of business was her family in?"

"Her mother owned a little diner in Barstow. It's halfway between here and Las Vegas."

Jack was dubious. "My first question is, I'd like to know how she socked away 12 million dollars owning a little diner in the desert?"

"Well, it's more like 36 million," Ben clarified. "Only the 12 are in question."

"Okay..." Jack raised an eyebrow. "I'm missing something, right?"

Ben leaned in conspiratorially. "Powerball."

It took Jack a moment to put it together. "The lottery?"

"That's right, Oregon 1998. 110-million-dollar jackpot, 55 million dollar lump sum payout."

Jack let out a whistle. "Jesus, that's a ton of money. But isn't it kind of a given that they blow some of it?"

"I don't know," Ben admitted, sliding Jack the file folder. "She's got a pretty good paper trail. Here's what the daughter gave me."

Jack wiped his mouth and eagerly scanned the ledger on top of the stack of documents, his brow furrowing in concentration as he tried to make sense of the complicated money trail.

Jack scanned the ledger, his brow furrowing as he tried to make sense of the large transactions. "Two checks...One for 1 million to Cristo Boating and one for 11 million to JTB Investments. That's a big check."

Ben nodded knowingly. "I looked into the Cristo Boating Company and it's out of business. It was located somewhere in Baja Mexico. That company has disappeared off the face of the earth."

"Must be one hell of a boat," Jack mused. "I guess at that price they're called ships, right?"

"Oh yeah, it's a ship alright," Ben said sardonically. "It would float with enough life jackets attached to it. Basically, it's worth a few thousand bucks. It's sitting behind the diner, just like the day it arrived. Besides, there's not any water to put it in for 300 miles in each direction."

Jack shook his head. "Sounds like someone saw her coming."

"Well maybe it's the same man?" Ben speculated.

But Jack was skeptical. "That doesn't make much sense. Usually, these guys take the money and run. Especially that much money, my God."

"That's where you come in," Ben said, leaning back. "Something's rotten here."

"You're right, something stinks," Jack agreed. "But the fact is it's gonna be tough to prove. The person who made the deals has passed, right? How do you get around that?"

Ben spreads his hands. "Look, she just wants to know who's behind it. We present the evidence and that's all. We're not prosecuting a case. We've got nothing to lose."

Seeing the potential payday, Jack asked, "So what's my end?"

"You actually find them and bring back the evidence and you walk away with 50 thousand."

Jack smiles impressed with the amount. "That's a lot of money. But what if I don't find anything concrete?"

"Expenses plus 20 thousand," Ben replied. "So, it's in your best interest to find this person and get the goods, if you know what I mean."

After mulling it over, Jack nodded. "Well...I'm game. Is everything in here?" He tapped the file folder.

"All she had," Ben confirmed. "Your best bet is to talk to Kathy Burns. She's still at the diner. It's easy to find."

Jack chuckled. "You think she would have sold that place after she won that money."

"Jack..." Ben gave him a look. "No, she bought the diner after she won. She moved from Oregon after she hit it. From what I was told, she bought that diner sight unseen."

That made Jack laugh out loud. "And they want me to find out 'why' the money vanished?"

Ben shrugged. "Frankly I don't care. To me it's a case, plain and simple. Get in and get it done, then we can both get paid."

"You're right, what the hell do I care?" Jack agreed readily. "Because to tell you the truth, I could really use this job right now."

Ben slid an envelope across the table. "That's five grand expense money. Do me a favor and keep your receipts."

"You got it." Jack pocketed the cash as they shook hands.

They stand up with Jack eager to get going.

"You take care now," Ben said.

"You do the same, and thanks."

Barstow California.

A day later, Jack pulled up in front of the "Come on In Café", squinting at the old diner in the desert sun. He checked the address against his notes, verifying he was in the right place. The newly painted building was nothing fancy, just a solitary outpost amid the dusty, barren landscape about 100 feet off the highway. The new neon sign glowed faintly even in the daylight.

"This is the million dollar restaurant, huh?" Jack muttered to himself as he climbed out of his car.

A bell rings on the door as Jack entered the near empty diner. "Good afternoon," the waitress called out.

"Good afternoon."

"Have a seat anywhere...I'll be with you in a moment."

Jack points to a corner booth "Thank you, I'll be right over here if you don't mind." Jack slid in and glanced around at the few regulars nursing cups of coffee. The interior looked newly renovated like it was brand new.

When the waitress came over with a menu and coffee pot. As she goes to pour a cup Jack says, "I better not, I had a couple big cups already. Sometimes that stuff keeps me up all night long."

The woman gave him a sly grin. "You're not trying to flirt with me, are you honey?"

Jack stammered defensively, "What, I was just saying…"

"I'm only playing...relax." The waitress winked. "How about I start you off with some water?"

Regaining his composure, Jack said, "Actually, I'm here to see Kathy Burns."

"Kathy, she's in the back. I'll tell her you're here." The waitress looked him over appraisingly. "What's your name?"

"Jack. Ah…Jack Peterson."

After she disappeared into the back, a woman emerged moments later, Kathy Burns, the owner. She was an attractive lady in her mid-forties, with a sweet Southern drawl. "You must be Mr. Peterson," she said, her voice rich with a thick accent.

Jack stood and shook her hand. "Please by all means call me Jack."

Kathy smiled warmly. "I thought you might be here a little later on in the day."

"Sometimes I can't sleep, so I started out earlier than I expected," Jack explained. "Not too early, am I?"

Kathy played down his concern. "Oh no, that's fine. You just missed our rush...well if you could call it that." She chuckled. "It's a pretty long drive for you."

"Not bad, it's a straight shot. That is if you miss the traffic," Jack replied.

"Traffic, oh, I forgot about that."

Jack couldn't help but notice her distinctive accent. "Where's that accent from? That doesn't sound like Oregon."

"Oh that," Kathy said with a warm smile. "I'm a Southern girl, more specifically Alabama."

Jack seems genuinely interested. "Your family from there?"

She nodded. "Yes, most of them still live there, but there ain't many of them left. I was the first to move on."

"I'm sorry to hear about your mother," Jack offered. "My condolences, it must be hard for you."

"Thank you," Kathy said softly. "I suppose it gets better with time. At least that's what they say. But every time I turn around in here, I run into her." She looked pensive. "Maybe that's good...I don't know."

"Ever think of selling?" Jack asked.

"Oh no," she replied adamantly. "This was momma's dream. A place of her own. I guess to understand that you had to understand momma."

Jack leaned back in the booth. "Do me a favor...tell me a little about her, so I can get an idea of the kind of woman she was."

Kathy settled in, reminiscing about her late mother. "Well, momma was a proud woman born and raised in Alabama, in the little town of Hazel Green, up by the Tennessee border. I don't think she ever went 200 miles in any direction her whole life. That is until she moved with me to Portland. She was married at 16 and I came about five years later. I was an only child."

"And your father?" Jack prompted gently.

Kathy looked down, wringing her hands as she composed herself. "Daddy..." She paused, then looked up with sadness in her eyes.

"I guess there's no easy way to say it. Daddy was a son of a bitch, a drunk and a womanizer. He was the one person who made my momma's life miserable. When he wasn't drunk raising hell at the house...He was in a bar fooling around."

Her voice took on a wistful tone as she vividly recalled her hardscrabble upbringing. "Momma swept a dirt floor until I was 7 and then we moved to a different house...at least this one had an outhouse. I remember when I was 14, she forced him to move us into a place with indoor plumbing." Kathy shook her head. "Well of course he raised hell again, got drunk and left for about a week, but she finally got us moved. She did that for me, she didn't want the high school kids to make fun of me. Of course, people were poor in those parts, but not like us, we were dirt poor. But she always made sure my clothes were clean and our house was neat and tidy."

Jack nodded slowly. "She sounds like one hell of a lady."

"She was..." Kathy said with pride. "The finest."

"So, where's your father now?"

A look of disdain crossed Kathy's face. "Five years ago, he was on a drunk. He had been gone a while from home."

"I used to tell momma to just leave him and come out with me. She took the whole 'death do us part' nonsense seriously. I would send her money. Sometimes she would send it back, but other times I knew she needed it, but she always kept track."

She sighed heavily. "Well, he run off with this woman to Tennessee and they were drunk coming back home from a bar and they tried to beat the train. They were killed right off.

It was bad enough he was killed, but how embarrassing it must have been for her. Well, he left enough money to bury him, but nothing else. I talked her into moving out with me. But she was getting on in years and the doctor said she needed a dry climate. I worked and saved up some, but it was gonna take some time..."

Kathy's eyes brightened as she got to the turn of events that changed everything. "But then she hit that jackpot and the rest, as they say, is history."

"It sounds like it couldn't have happened to a nicer person," Jack said sincerely.

Kathy nodded fervently. "Oh...we prayed for a miracle and the good lord answered our prayers."

"Did she play often?" Jack asked.

"Gamble? No... heavens no. Momma never gambled in her life," Kathy replied, shaking her head. "That was the first...and as she would say, the last time."

Jack leaned back, stunned. "That's amazing, I've never heard anything like that! She won one of the biggest jackpots ever on her very first-time gambling?"

Kathy smiled at his reaction. "It's hard to believe, but that's the truth."

"Wow," Jack said, impressed. "Go on..."

"She gets that check and subscribes to every newspaper in the Western United States, "I mean we get about 20 papers a day. She reads the classified of every one of them. One day she finds this ad listing this diner and buys it over the phone. Compared to what money she had; it wasn't that much. But like she said, 'Sweetie, it's all ours.' I moved with her, mainly to keep an eye on her."

Kathy paused, her voice cracking with emotion. "She died in her sleep about two months ago. That's when I started looking at her books. Like I said, she used to keep track of everything. Those amounts weren't like her. She wrote big checks for sure, but they were mainly to charity. The only thing she really got for herself is this diner."

"We are talking about a lady who left a drawer full of freshly cut coupons behind. Of course, she bought some new clothes, a car and a TV or two but nothing like that boat. My God, she's never even been on the water."

"And the investment?" Jack prompted.

Kathy shook her head in bewilderment. "Now that makes no sense, if she wanted to make money, she wouldn't have bought this place. I've got a whole box of stuff I want you to look at."

Not wanting to pry too much, Jack said carefully, "Don't take this the wrong way but I have to know. How come you never knew what was going on, you were right here?"

To his surprise, Kathy didn't take offense. "That's a fair question. You have to understand this: Momma was happy for probably the first time in her life. She had more money than you could shake a stick at. When I saw that boat roll in here, I thought 'what the hell is she doing?'

Tears welled up in Kathy's eyes as she explained, "But if you would have seen the look on her face...It was...it was like she saw an angel. What the hell did I care? But after seeing all this it kills me that someone might have took advantage of her. I want to know it was for something good. I want to know momma wasn't taken for a fool."

Jack could see the desperation in her eyes. "I'm getting a better picture now," he assured her gently.

Kathy composed herself before asking, "And can I ask about who Jack is? Tell me a little about yourself."

His body language was dismissive. "Me... oh nothing much to tell. You'd get bored."

But Kathy was insistent. "That's okay, go on. I'd like to know who's working on momma's case."

Jack relented with a sigh. "Well, I spent 26 years in the police force and retired early. I started this private investigation agency right after that and I've been doing it for a few years."

"Married?" Kathy asked.

Jack's expression clouded briefly. "Once and it lasted about 10 years. Separated for a long while. We never officially divorced. She died about 9 years ago."

"I'm sorry," Kathy said sympathetically. "Did you have any kids?"

Jack shifted uncomfortably in his seat. "Yes...one. A boy, he's 29 and lives in Los Angeles. We don't see each other as much as I'd like but...you know."

"I don't mean to pry," Kathy said quickly.

But Jack dismissed her concern. "No, no... that's fine. We had a falling out some years back. I've tried a couple times, but he's as stubborn as his old man I guess."

"It's never too late," Kathy offered kindly.

A melancholy look came over Jack's face. "That's what I keep telling myself, but the truth is we never know how long we've got."

Kathy nodded somberly. "That's so true..."

Clearing his throat. "Oh, I catch up with him every couple of weeks but it's just idle chit-chat. I guess that's my fault, but that's a long story. They sat silently for a few moments.

"Hey, I don't mean to change the subject, but we ought to get to that evidence you have."

"You see I get someone to talk to and I just jabber on," Kathy fretted. "I didn't mean to pry."

Jack assured her, "No... That's okay, I haven't talked about it in a while. I'm fine..."

"Alright, let's get to that box," Kathy said, rising from the booth.

Later, Jack and Kathy emerged from the diner, he is carrying a small box of paperwork and other items Kathy had collected relating to her mother's curious dealings. They stopped outside the doorway.

"Thank you, Mr. Peterson," Kathy said warmly. "It's been a pleasure."

"I want to thank you for sharing your mother's story with me," Jack replied. "You were lucky to have such a fine mother. And please, call me Jack."

Kathy smiled and nodded. "Okay Jack, I appreciate everything you're doing. Keep in touch and you take care now."

"You do the same and I'll call you as soon as I get some info," Jack promised.

"Well, I'll be here," Kathy said wistfully. "What else am I going to do?"

Jack regarded her shrewdly. "You don't have to stay."

But Kathy shook her head. "No, I have to, at least for a while."

Understanding flickered in Jack's eyes. "I understand..."

As he turned to leave, Jack stopped abruptly. "Hey, where the heck's that boat?"

"Oh, that old thing, it's around back," Kathy replied dismissively. "I don't know what I'm going to do with it. Drive around and you'll see...you can't miss it."

"Will do," Jack said with a nod.

Jack got in his car and drove around back, stopping when he spotted the old boat peeking out from under a canvas tarp. It was about 40 feet long, an all wood vessel painted white, peeling badly and had clearly seen better days. In its current neglected condition, there was no way it was seaworthy. Sitting tilted askew on the ground, perched on some wooden stands with no trailer. It looked completely out of place in the desert.

Jack got out and paced around the boat, snapping photographs from various angles with an instant camera. He stopped at the stern and pulled back a tarp to reveal the name painted on the hull.

"Salvation...huh," he muttered to himself, studying the peeling lettering. Jack stepped back and took a few more pictures before shaking his head and returning to his car.

Chapter Three

~ Kingman ~

That evening found Jack reviewing the evidence Kathy had provided at his hotel room in Las Vegas. Papers and documents were spread out on the table and bed as he sorted through them, taking notes. He paused on one particular item that catches his attention.

"JTB Investments, Kingman Arizona," he read aloud. "How did she decide on that company and where the hell is Kingman?"

Jack pulled out a map and jotted down the details before picking up the phone. "Ben?"

"Jack, how's it going?" the lawyer answered.

"Good, really good," Jack replied.

"Did you get to talk to Kathy?"

"Earlier today at the restaurant."

"How did that go?"

A smile crept across Jack's face. "Good...I got some nice leads. I was going to tell you I'm heading to Kingman, Arizona tomorrow. It should only take a couple hours."

"Couple hours?" Ben sounded surprised. "Where the hell are you?"

"Vegas," Jack admitted sheepishly.

Ben laughed. "Not spending all that expense money."

"Oh, hell no, I haven't placed a bet in years," Jack assured him.

"Sounds like a story," Ben prodded.

But Jack dismissed him. "Yeah, but a real boring one. Say, I've got a lead at that one place, JTB Investments. You ever heard of them before?"

"No, well...not until I saw that file."

"Sounds fishy to me," Jack said with a frown.

"Like I said, this one is pretty interesting."

Jack couldn't argue with that assessment. "You weren't wrong about that. Tell you what, I'll give you a call tomorrow from Kingman if I find out anything."

"That will be fine, I'll talk to you then," Ben agreed.

"You do the same," Jack said, then added, "Oh Ben..."

"Yeah..."

"That boat, it was just like you described...a real piece of junk."

Ben chuckled. "I hear that, it's no ship. Talk to you later."

"Bye now..."

The next morning found Jack peering through the windows of JTB Investments' office in downtown Kingman, Arizona. The place was deserted, the bare office containing just a simple oak desk and phone. The company name stenciled on the door.

As Jack moved on to check out the neighboring barbershop, an elderly man with a wiry build and weathered features approached. "Can I help you?" the newcomer asked gruffly.

Turning, Jack replied, "This your shop?" He pointed through the window.

"Yes, it is..." The man sized up Jack appraisingly. "Haircut?"

Jack ran a hand self-consciously over his thinning hair. "No, not today I'm trying to keep what's left."

The old timer smirked and gave him a look over. "I've seen worse, you're all right."

Extending his hand, Jack introduced himself. "My name's Jack Peterson."

"Nathan Pruitt, but everyone calls me Slim," the barber replied, shaking Jack's hand firmly.

"Okay, Slim it is...Call me Jack."

"So, what can I do for you?" Slim asked in a no-nonsense tone.

"Just wondering about your neighbors here, JTB Investments," Jack explained.

Slim jerked a thumb towards his shop. "You mind if we talk while I get things going?"

"That's fine," Jack agreed, following him inside.

As Slim began his morning routine of raising the blinds and prepping his supplies, he said, "What do you want to know?"

"How long they been there?"

Slim shrugged. "I suppose they moved in about 5 years ago. But you wouldn't even know he was there."

"How so?" Jack pressed.

"I've only seen that fella...Oh, about 8 times," the barber estimated. "I suppose he travels a lot, he's got a funny accent."

That piqued Jack's interest. "Funny like what? What I mean is, where from?"

"He's English or one of those countries..." Slim puts his finger to his temple. "Sorry, I'm not good with accents."

"White guy?" Jack asked for clarification.

"Yeah..." Slim nodded.

"You talk to him?"

The barber shrugged. "Well, I cut his hair a couple times."

"What's his name?"

Slim squinted, trying to recall. "I think it's John, but I tell you, it's getting harder to remember names. Is he in some trouble?"

Jack dismisses the idea. "No, the reason I'm asking is that I've been trying to get a hold of them for an investment opportunity."

Slim chuckled matter-of-factly. "Good luck."

"Why do you say that?"

"I've asked him about investing some," the old man explained. "I've got a nice nest egg socked away and he told me he would let me know when something good came up, but I never heard a word."

Jack arched an eyebrow. "That's kind of strange."

But Slim didn't seem fazed. "Mr. I've seen a lot of strange things cutting hair for 40 years. That's not anywhere close to the strangest. I suppose he's busy, he's never around."

"Do you know how I can get a hold of him?"

"No, I don't." Slim admitted. "You could try the owner of this building, though?"

Jack perked up at that suggestion. "Do you have the number?"

"Sure, no problem." Slim handed him a business card from the counter. "Go ahead and keep that, I got a couple of them."

"Thanks for your help," Jack said, pocketing the card.

"Let me know if you find anything good."

"I'll do that."

As Jack headed back to his car, he pulled out his phone and thumbed through the contacts to his sister Susan's number. Settling in behind the wheel, he called her at the IRS office where she worked.

The automated message prompted, "Press one and the number if you know your party's extension."

Jack did so, then waited as the call went through.

"Susan Davis, can I help you?" his sister's familiar voice answered.

"Sue, how the heck are you doing?" Jack said warmly.

"Jack?" There was a smile in her voice. "Wow, long time no hear. How are you?"

"I can't complain," he replied, "then again who would listen?"

Susan laughed at his joke. "Wow, this is a surprise."

"So how's everything?" Jack asked.

"Fine," Susan said knowingly. "You must be on a case, right?"

Jack feigned innocence. "How did you know?"

"Because...you called me?" she teased.

"Is it that obvious?"

"Yes, you're terrible," Susan chided affectionately. "You should call more often."

Jack sighed. "I know, I get so busy though. How's the family?"

"Everyone is great," Susan replied. "How is Shawn doing?"

A pause, then, "He's fine, I talked to him a week ago."

"You and your son are going to drive me nuts," Susan lamented. "Why are you both so pig-headed?"

Sensing a lecture, Jack deflected, "Come on, Sue, let's not start when we were getting along so well."

"Okay, I'll stop preaching but consider it, okay?" his sister relented. "All right, I'll make it easy. What can I get for you?"

Jack chuckled. "You see, you're the best. That's why I call."

"No Jack," Susan corrected him. "You call because I work here."

"Ouch..."

"Just like when we were kids, right?" she teased.

Playing along, Jack protested, "No... Hell no, you were mean."

"With three brothers you have to be," Susan said straightforwardly.

After a moment, Jack got down to business. "Okay, the name of the company is JTB Investments in Kingman, Arizona."

Susan jotted down the details. "So what's the problem?"

"I've got a client that invested a considerable amount of money and hasn't seen a return," Jack explained vaguely.

"What happened to the divorce cases?" Susan asked curiously.

Jack hedged, "Ah, this just fell in my lap."

His sister didn't pry further. "Tell you what, I'll run the check and email you what I find, same address?"

"Yes, same one forever," Jack confirmed with a chuckle.

"You're one big creature of habit," Susan teased.

Jack laughed. "Well, it's so hard to change."

"You best keep in touch or this is the last one," Susan mock threatened.

"I promise...no more excuses."

"It was nice hearing from you," she said sincerely.

"I will, talk to you later."

"Bye..."

After hanging up, Jack drove up the road to the nearest gas station to refuel and see what other information he could glean about the mysterious JTB Investments and its elusive owner. As the young attendant filled his tank, Jack made casual conversation.

"Say, where's a good place to stay in town?"

"Well, there's Roadside Inn up this street about a mile and the Motel 6 up on 40," the kid replied.

Jack nodded, looking around as he spoke. "Say you ever heard of JTB Investments up the street by the barber shop?"

The attendant's face registered recognition. "Yeah, that fella with the sports car runs it?"

That piqued Jack's interest. "Sports car, what kind?"

"I think he's partial to Corvettes," the young man said. "He's had a couple of them. Last time I saw him he had a silver one."

Trying not to seem too eager, Jack asked, "Do you know his name?"

The attendant eyed him warily. "He in some trouble?"

"No, just business," Jack assured him.

Seemingly satisfied, the attendant replied, "Well I don't know his last name but his first is John. He's not around that much."

Jack made a mental note of that tidbit. "That's what I hear. Thanks for the information."

After paying, Jack got a room at the Roadside Inn the attendant had recommended. That evening, he pored over his notes from Kingman and booted up his laptop to check his email, clicking on the message from his sister Susan at the IRS.

The phone rang. "This is Jack," he answered.

"Jack, it's Sue," came his sister's voice. "I have some information for you."

"Go ahead, shoot," Jack said, pen poised to take notes.

"I sent it all to you, but I can probably explain it better over the phone," Susan offered.

"Okay."

She began reciting the details she had uncovered. "JTB Investments is owned by a Mr. John Smith."

Jack snorted derisively. "That sounds phony."

"Wait it gets better," Susan said ironically. "JTB has only 4 shareholders three in the United States, one in Canada. Officially they invest in mines in South America, but from what I can tell they just lose money every year. They haven't turned a profit in the 5 years they've been in business."

Jack leaned back, digesting this new information as Susan continued. "John Smith is a British citizen and other than that I don't have anything on him. I did a little checking and here's the weird part: JTB's three clients from the US have all won the lottery and within 6 months made a large investment into JTB."

His ears perked up. "You're kidding..."

"I sent you their names," Susan confirmed. "Here's the scoop on the three US investors, get this: one is Arizona Armando Diaz; a woman from

Barstow, California named Katie Burns; and the last one is Henry Riddell of Sweetwater, Texas. Total deposits of around 36 million dollars."

Jack let out a low whistle as he scribbled furiously. "Did it say what they invested in?"

There was a pause as Susan presumably checked her notes. "Not specifically, just listed as various unspecified investments."

"Probably code for something shady," Jack muttered.

Susan cleared her throat. "Well, that's about all I could dig up without going through official channels, if you know what I mean."

"I hear you, sis," Jack assured her. "This is great, you really came through for me."

"Anything for my big brother," Susan replied fondly. "Just be careful out there. And keep in touch this time, you hear?"

Jack smiled at her sisterly concern. "You know it. Thanks again, Sue."

"Be careful, Jack," Susan warned. "People will do just about anything over that amount of money."

Jack chuckled dismissively. "Don't worry, I'll be fine. I used to be a cop, you know."

But his sister wasn't appeased. "But remember you're not a cop anymore, so be careful."

"Okay...okay, just kidding," Jack relented.

"Call me," Susan insisted.

"Alright, take care."

"Bye."

After hanging up, Jack stared at the papers and printouts strewn across the motel desk, deep in thought. "Well..." he muttered to himself. "Let's find out who the hell you are."

He logged onto the internet and began running searches on "John Smith", quickly realizing how common the name was. Switching tactics, Jack accessed a private investigator database service and started cross-referencing details like the man's British citizenship, business connections to JTB Investments, and various other data points his sister had provided. He spent hours compiling information and taking meticulous notes late into the evening.

The next morning, Jack placed a call to Ben Klein, the lawyer who had hired him.

"Hello?" Ben answered.

"Ben, it's Jack."

"Well where are you now, Paris?" Ben quipped.

Jack chuckled. "No, still in Kingman. But it feels like Paris."

"Yeah, I bet. What's up?"

"His name is John Smith," Jack stated.

Ben didn't seem impressed. "Oh...That narrows it down."

"I know what you mean," Jack admitted, "but I think I actually have it narrowed down. He's British and according to what I've found, that's his birth name. Funny thing is this guy even shows up to pay his traffic tickets."

"He's either fearless or stupid," Ben mused.

Jack shrugged, though Ben couldn't see it. "I don't know just yet, but here's the deal. They took in about 37 to 40 million in revenue over the last 5 years. Zero returns. Get this, all the shareholders are lottery winners."

"What..." Ben sounded stunned. "All of them?"

"Yes, one's an actual priest Father Armando Diaz; a rancher named Henry Riddell; and then our client. The odd thing is, not one complaint."

"I didn't expect that much money, Jack," Ben said, the wheels clearly turning. "That's pretty big..."

Jack nodded. "It is. I'm heading to Nogales, Arizona to see Father Diaz. I want to see what he has to say."

"Better than a stakeout, right?" Ben joked. "But do me a favor, watch your back. You know what that kind of money means."

"I hear you," Jack replied soberly. "Someone else told me that."

"Keep in touch," Ben instructed.

"I will. Talk to you later."

After hanging up, Jack hit the road, cruising down the highway while digesting everything he'd learned so far, the radio playing faintly in the background. His first stop was the St. John Vianney Orphanage in Nogales, seeking an audience with Father Armando Diaz.

Jack pulled up and parked in front of the old but well maintained building, eyeing the "Office" sign before heading inside. A courteous nun greeted him.

"Good afternoon, can I help you?"

"Good afternoon, yes you can," Jack replied easily. "I'm looking for Father Armando Diaz. I called earlier this morning."

The nun's expression was politely skeptical. "Do you have an appointment?"

"No..." Jack admitted. "But I think he's expecting me."

"What is your name?"

"Jack Peterson."

"Have a seat and I'll see if he's free," she said, already turning away.

"Thank you."

As Jack settled into one of the chairs, he glanced around the office at the various religious icons and emblems, seeming vaguely uncomfortable amidst the trappings of faith. Before long, the nun returned.

"He'll see you now, go right in through that door."

"Thank you." Jack rose and made his way to Father Diaz's office, giving a polite rap before entering.

Armando Diaz looked to be in his late 30s, a fit Latino man whose clerical attire befitted his vocation. "Mr. Peterson, is it?" he greeted Jack, standing and extending his hand.

Jack shook it firmly. "Yes, thank you for seeing me on such short notice. I know you're probably a busy man."

"Yes, there is always work to do," Father Diaz replied humbly.

Jack glanced around as he said, "This is an orphanage? I didn't think they had orphanages in this day and age."

"As long as people have children, there will be some who have nowhere to go," the priest explained patiently. "You're right though, most of them are foster children or live in group homes, but they are without families none the less."

Eyeing the aging structure, Jack remarked, "This place looks pretty old."

"It's been here for over a hundred years in one form or another," Father Diaz said with evident pride. "Hopefully one day, there will be no use for it...at least it's in my prayers."

Jack nodded slowly. "Have you worked here long?"

"Sixteen years," the priest replied. "It was my first assignment and I guess it just fit me."

Father Diaz continues with a sense of pride. "I remember walking in that front door and realizing I was home. This place is as much a part of me as an arm or a leg now."

"Sounds like you found the perfect job," Jack commented.

Father Diaz smiled wistfully. "Funny you said that my grandfather used to tell me to find out what I love to do and then find someone to pay me to do it. Then I would never have to work again."

Jack returned the warm smile. "Well...then you're a lucky man."

"Yes," the priest agreed. "I've been quite fortunate."

Jack decided it was time to get down to business. "Father, I don't want to take up a bunch of your time, so I'll get right to the point. I'm working on a case for a client, well more like an investigation of some questionable holdings. The original shareholder has passed on..."

"I'm sorry to hear that..." Father Diaz said sincerely.

"Yes, it's a shame," Jack continued, "because from what I've heard she was a really nice lady. Oddly enough, you and this client have invested large amounts of money in the same company; JTB Investments. You did invest with them, didn't you?"

The priest nodded calmly. "Yes, I did. Is there some problem?"

"Let me tell you what I find odd," Jack said frankly. "I can't find a single shareholder who's made a dime or filed a single complaint. That sounds rather odd to me."

Father Diaz seemed unperturbed. "Well, some investments do take more time than others."

Jack pressed on. "That's true...Is it true you also won the lottery?"

Another nod. "Yes, it is."

"When did that happen?"

"January 1998."

"Did you play a lot?" Jack asked curiously.

The priest shook his head. "Not really, I buy a ticket every now and then."

Jack leaned forward intently. "Do you mind if I ask what you did with the rest of the money?"

"No, I don't mind," Father Diaz replied equably. "It went here for repairs and to the needy. As far as me, I don't need much, all that I require is provided."

Jack raised an eyebrow skeptically. "Tell me if I'm wrong, but doesn't it seem strange that two lottery winners would invest in the same company?"

Father Diaz considered this calmly. "Well, maybe a little."

"And how about three lottery winners?" Jack pressed.

The priest nodded slowly. "That might seem odd."

"That's what I thought," Jack said, leaning back.

But Father Diaz didn't seem overly concerned. "But although it's odd...I don't see where it's something to be concerned about. That is...I'm not complaining."

"But one person is concerned and at least wants some answers," Jack explained.

Understanding dawned on the priest's face. "One of the investors?"

"No, the beneficiary of the estate has some concerns," Jack clarified. "She's the person I was hired by."

Father Diaz nodded slowly. "So, what you're saying is she's concerned she hasn't had a return on the investment?"

"That." Jack confirmed, "and there is another large purchase that doesn't make much sense, but that's a whole other story. But I keep going back to the three lottery winners because it's not something that would happen on its own...like a coincidence."

The priest stroked his chin thoughtfully. "I suppose you're right. But this world works in many strange ways. Some cannot truly be explained."

Jack looked intrigued. "I'm not following?"

"What I mean is we are sometimes brought together by other forces," Father Diaz said simply.

Realization dawned on Jack's face and he pointed upwards with a smile. "You mean the big guy?" Jack points up.

Father Diaz met his gaze levelly. "I believe God plays a part in all things."

Jack considered this, then said, "Tell me if you would, how did you come to make that investment?"

"I was approached with the idea," the priest replied.

"By John Smith?" Jack verified.

Father Diaz nodded. "Yes, Mr. Smith asked if I would be interested in a business opportunity."

"And you just handed over your money?" Jack asked incredulously.

But the priest shook his head. "I wouldn't say that, because it actually wasn't my money."

Jack furrowed his brow in confusion. "Come again?"

"What I mean is it wasn't mine to begin with," Father Diaz clarified.

Jack smirked. "I can see that...A philosophical approach to investing." He inquisitively continued. "But what convinced you to go with him?"

The priest considered his words carefully. "It was a feeling I had...That the money would be used to its fullest and I trusted Mr. Smith."

"Did you know him long?" Jack asked pointedly.

"Not too long," Father Diaz admitted. "A few weeks."

Jack let out a short laugh of disbelief. "You knew him a few weeks and decided to write a six million dollar check?"

But the priest remained unruffled. "I felt comfortable with Mr. Smith, it's hard to explain."

"That's a lot of faith, Father..." Jack couldn't help but observe sardonically.

Father Diaz smiled serenely. "Well, faith is our business."

Jack had to chuckle at that, pointing an acknowledging finger at the priest. "You got me there..."

"I'm sorry, Mr. Peterson," Father Diaz said regretfully, rising from his chair. "I wish we had more time, but I have a class to teach. Walk with me and we can finish our conversation."

As they strolled down the hallway, Jack asked, "Do you have a number to get ahold of Mr. Smith?"

"Only the office number in Kingman..." the priest replied. "Do you have that?"

Jack nodded. "Yes, I have his office number. Is that how you keep up with him?"

"Mr. Smith calls me periodically."

"Has he called recently?"

Father Diaz confirmed, "Yes, as a matter of fact, he called just last week."

Pulling out a business card, Jack handed it over. "Could you tell him I'd like to talk to him if he calls again? Here's my card."

"I'll be sure to do that," Father Diaz promised, pocketing the card.

"Well, thank you for your time, Father," Jack said sincerely. "It's been enlightening, to say the least."

The priest smiled humbly. "I'm glad I could be of some help."

They shook hands as Father Diaz opened the classroom door. Jack's gaze was immediately drawn to the chalkboard, where the letters "JTB" were circled prominently.

"Say, Father," he said with an amused smile. "You're not trying to drum up some business, are you?"

Following Jack's eyes to the board, Father Diaz chuckled. "How so?"

"Well, you have those letters circled on the board," Jack pointed out.

The priest looked at Jack inquisitively. "Oh that...Are you familiar with the Bible?"

Jack shrugged. "I've read it some in Sunday school, but it's been a while."

"Well then you know there is the Apostle John and John the Baptist," Father Diaz explained patiently. "That's how we differentiate between the two."

Jack raised his eyebrows in dawning realization. "So JTB Investments stands for John the Baptist?"

"To tell you the truth, I never thought of it that way," the priest admitted with a laugh. "What a coincidence."

"Yes, another coincidence," Jack echoed inquisitively.

Father Diaz smiled widely. "Yes indeed, it's a small world."

Jack couldn't argue with that assessment. "That's an understatement."

They shook hands once more as the priest said, "Well, good day Mr. Peterson. Take care."

"Thank you, Father. You do the same."

Jack had only made it halfway down the hall when Father Diaz called out, "Mr. Peterson!"

He turned to see the priest striding towards him. "Yes, Father?"

"Could I ask, what was the other large purchase that's in question?"

Having almost forgotten about that detail, Jack replied, "A boat, a really expensive boat, with a rather strange name."

"What was the name?"

Jack met the priest's guileless gaze steadily. "Salvation."

Father Diaz looked momentarily taken aback. "That is an odd name for a boat."

"Yes, it is," Jack agreed understatedly. "Especially that boat. Good day, Father..."

As he turned to leave once more, Father Diaz's voice rang out loudly. "You know what the Bible says?"

Intrigued despite himself, Jack paused and looked back over his shoulder and turned. "No, what's that?"

The priest spoke two simple words: "It lies within."

Jack's brow furrowed in confusion for a beat before realization spread across his face. "What does?"

Father Diaz called out the answer with a smile: "Salvation!"

Jack had to grin at that, shaking his head in amusement as he pointed a finger at the priest. "Yes, I've heard that, Father. Thank you..."

With a warm laugh, Father Diaz disappeared into his classroom as Jack chuckled and made his way outside, mulling over their thought-provoking conversation.

<u>Chapter Four</u>

~ Sunsets ~

That evening back at the motel, Jack thumbed through his notes before picking up the phone and dialing Kathy's number.

When she answered, Jack said warmly, "Hello, this is Jack Peterson."

"Jack, how are you?" came Kathy's welcoming voice.

"I'm pretty good, and yourself?"

"Good...some news?" Kathy asked hopefully.

Jack nodded. "That's why I'm calling. I'll tell you what, this case has a few twists and turns in it already. I'm not sure I know the half of it just yet."

"How's that?"

"Well, I tracked down our man his name is John Smith and by all accounts he's legit, but I haven't actually talked with him yet," Jack explained. "Now brace yourself...All Mr. Smith's shareholders also won the lottery...well 3 of them and I don't know about the 4th, he's a Canadian. All told, 37 million dollars in revenue and zero returns."

Kathy sounded stunned. "Nobody's received anything?"

"Zilch...nada...nothing," Jack confirmed. "The strange part is I just met with Father Diaz, another investor, and he doesn't seem all that worried about his six million dolllar check."

"Father Diaz...six million?" Kathy repeated in disbelief.

Jack nodded, though she couldn't see. "Yes, a real priest. That's why it doesn't add up, I don't see anything illegal, but everything isn't on the up and up. I can't make heads or tails of what's going on just yet."

"This Father Diaz also won the lottery?"

"Yep, 1999. 26 million cash payout, just like your mom, and just like Henry Riddell," Jack said, ticking them off on his fingers. "And oddly enough, just like Mr. John Smith."

Kathy sounded incredulous. "John Smith is also a lottery winner? This is too crazy...and Henry Riddell, who's he?"

"Henry is a cattle rancher in Sweetwater, Texas," Jack clarified. "He's the most recent. He won about 8 months ago and invested soon after. He's my next stop."

"Where are you now?" Kathy asked.

"Nogales, Arizona."

"Wow, you're sure on a mission," she remarked.

Jack chuckled. "It feels like one. I'll tell you what, this case is pretty interesting."

"Are you getting closer?"

"Yes and no," Jack hedged. "Yes, because I have the person nailed down. And no because I don't see an actual crime yet. People lose millions in the stock market every day and nobody can do a thing about that. I need to find some fraud for anything to stick."

Kathy sounded relieved. "Great job so far, keep me posted will you?"

"Sure, I'll do that," Jack promised. "And do me a favor, tell me if Mr. Smith happens to call. He seems to keep up for some reason."

"I'll do that, and you take care," Kathy said.

"You too and I'll talk to you later. Bye now."

That night at the motel, Jack tossed and turned, haunted by a vivid dream taking him back to the painful dissolution of his marriage years earlier.

He was going to pick up his then 14 year old son Shawn for their scheduled visitation, hurriedly pulling up to Margaret's house and trying to straighten his clothes after once again running late. Before he could even knock, Margaret stepped out to head him off.

"Sorry I'm a little late, my plans got all screwed up," Jack apologized gruffly.

Margaret's expression was troubled. "Jack, let's talk out here."

Seeing the writing on the wall, Jack braced himself. "Listen I'm sorry, I'm a lousy 45 minutes late."

"It's not that," Margaret said heavily. "He doesn't want to go today."

Jack looked stricken. "What do you mean? I talked to him just yesterday."

"He can't tell you anything, he's afraid you'll get mad," Margaret said carefully.

"Jesus Christ..." Jack raked a hand through his hair in frustration before admitting, "Okay, let me talk to him. I'll straighten it out."

But his ex-wife refused to budge. "No, not today. He's very confused right now."

"Come on, can I catch a lousy break?" Jack protested angrily.

Margaret stood firm. "It's not about you, Jack. It doesn't always have to be about you."

"I got these tickets special for him, everything is all set," Jack insisted stubbornly.

His ex-wife gave him a pitying look. "Set for you, Jack. He doesn't even like football."

Scoffing, Jack asked derisively, "Now he doesn't like football? What are you doing, turning him into a fruitcake?"

The slap came out of nowhere, snapping Jack's head to the side. He stood there stunned as Margaret glared at him, chest heaving with angry breaths. After an endless moment, Jack found his voice.

"What the hell you do that for? I wasn't serious. So he's a little sensitive..."

"Making comments like that is only going to hurt him more," Margaret said, her voice shaking with emotion. "What are you going to do, teach him the right way to live, like you? No matter what he is, he's my son. He's your son."

Jack tried a different tack. "Let me talk to him and we can work this out."

But Margaret was adamant. "There is nothing to work out. He's not sick and he doesn't need to be fixed. Face it, you and he are very different and until you stop trying to make him into you, you're always going to have problems."

His frustration boiling over, Jack threw up his hands. "So that's it, I have no say?"

"There is nothing to decide, that's where you don't get it, Jack," Margaret shot back. "You're detached from the rest of us, you only see what you want to."

Fed up, Jack turned on his heel. "I'm getting the hell out of here, tell him to call me when he's ready! I've got a game to go to."

Margaret called after him desperately. "If you don't try to understand him, you'll lose him!"

Jack whirled around, hurt and anger warring in his expression. "So, what am I supposed to do?"

Her voice was sad but resolute. "You'll have to figure that out, Jack. I can't help you there, you do what you have to. For once...do all you can."

Inside, young Shawn had heard snatches of the heated argument, and watched somberly through the window as his father's car pulled away...

Later that night, Jack sat alone at his kitchen table, a half empty bottle of whiskey and the unused football tickets in front of him. Taking a long pull straight from the bottle, he grimaced as the harsh liquor burned its way down. Setting the bottle down heavily, he picked up one of the tickets and stared at it for a long moment before ripping it in half violently.

He lit a cigarette and took a deep drag, letting the acrid smoke fill his lungs before exhaling slowly. As the smoke dissipated, he dropped the torn ticket into the ash tray and used his lighter to set it smoldering. Watching it slowly burn to cinders, Jack drained his glass and poured another, then stumbled over to the window. He yanked the cord, raising the blinds to reveal the dying light of sunset. But after gazing out for only a few seconds, he abruptly released the cord, plunging the room back into darkness.

The dream faded to black as Jack awoke with a start in the present-day motel room. He sat on the edge of the bed, running a hand over his weary face. After a few moments, he reached into his pants pocket and pulled out his wallet, extracting the only two photos he kept one of his son Shawn, and one of his late ex-wife Margaret from happier times.

Studying Margaret's smiling face, Jack spoke out loud to the empty room, his voice gruff with melancholy. "You were always smarter than I was, Margaret. I just didn't get it. I wish I could have told you that." He managed a sad smile. "Typical Jack, right?"

The next morning, Jack mustered his courage and dialed a very familiar number from the motel room his son Shawn's phone in Los Angeles. When Shawn answered, Jack forced a casual tone.

"Hey Shawn, it's your dad."

"Hey," Shawn replied, sounding slightly awkward.

"How you feeling?" Jack asked.

"Pretty good, the same."

Jack hesitated before pushing forward. "I was thinking about coming to see you this week. Are you busy?"

"Me? No, I don't have any plans," Shawn said.

"I guess it's a date then," Jack tried to sound upbeat.

"Just let me know when."

"Sure, I'll do that." Jack scrambled for more to say. "Well...I guess I'll talk to you then. You take care."

"Yeah, you too. Bye..."

As Jack hung up the phone, he was immediately disgusted with himself. "God damn it...I can never say what I mean."

In a sudden burst of self-loathing, he angrily kicked over the chair, agitating himself further as memories of past failures swirled in his mind.

Later that day, Jack left a message on Henry Riddell's answering machine. "Mr. Riddell, this is Jack Peterson of Peterson Investigations. If you could please give me a call when you get in, I'd appreciate it. My number is area code 619-555-3696. Thank you."

Unknown to Jack, Henry was actually home and overheard the message as it was being left. He immediately picked up the phone and placed a call.

"Hello?" came the accented voice on the other end.

"Mr. Smith, it's me Henry Riddell," the rancher said.

"Good to hear from you, Henry," John Smith replied warmly. "How are you today?"

"Fine sir. Jack Peterson just called me."

Smith's tone sharpened with interest. "Did he now...And what did he have to say?"

"He left a message on my machine; I didn't speak to him directly."

"Well, it seems Mr. Peterson has done his homework," Smith commented.

"What would you like me to do, Mr. Smith?" Henry asked obediently.

"Nothing at the moment," Smith replied calmly. "I get the feeling that you're getting close to providing that service we talked about."

Henry didn't question it. "Anything you want, Mr. Smith...just ask."

"Keep me posted, Henry. And take care now."

"You do the same, sir."

A short while later, Jack pulled into the parking lot of Kelly's Liquors, a small neighborhood bottle shop. As he wandered the aisles, his gaze kept getting drawn to the shelves of whiskey, vodka and other hard liquors behind the counter. He grabbed a soda from the cooler and got in line but remained distracted by the tempting array of bottles.

"That it?" the cashier asked brusquely when it was Jack's turn.

Lost in thought, Jack didn't immediately respond until the clerk repeated louder, "Hey fella, is that it?"

Jack tore his eyes away. "Yeah," he mumbled.

But at the last second, his resolve crumbled. "Wait...give me a fifth of Jack."

The cashier didn't bat an eye. "Gotcha."

As Jack paid and walked back to his car, he berated himself under his breath. "Son of a bitch, why in the hell did I do that?"

He looked at the brown paper bag clutched in his hand; the outline of the bottle visible. "Let's put you somewhere safe."

Jack popped the trunk and tossed the bagged bottle inside, slamming it shut forcefully. "Can't do any damage from there, can you?"

He patted the trunk lid halfheartedly before getting behind the wheel and driving off, regretting his moment of weakness already.

A few hours later found Jack in the small Texas town of Sweetwater, pulling up to Vicky's Restaurant in search of information on Henry Riddell. As the friendly waitress approached with menus, she asked cheerfully, "Alone?"

"Unfortunately, yes." Jack replied.

The waitress smiled knowingly. "Sometimes it's nice to eat alone."

But Jack just shook his head. "Well, I do it far too often."

"That's not good," she chided gently, leading him to a cozy booth. "I have a booth right over here, how's that?"

"That will do fine, thank you," Jack said gratefully, taking a seat.

"Here's your menu, I'll be back in a minute," the waitress said before bustling off.

Left alone with his thoughts for the moment, Jack stared unseeingly out the window, a pensive expression on his careworn face as years of regret seemed to weigh on him all at once. Slipping on his reading glasses, he tried to shake off the melancholy by studying the menu, his mood shifting as he pulled himself together.

When the waitress returned, she eyed him appraisingly. "Well, you got it figured out?"

Jack let out a good-natured chuckle. "Life or just this order?"

She played along with a grin. "Well, if you've got life figured out honey, I'll take a seat!"

"No, you got the wrong guy for that," Jack deflected self-deprecatingly. "I'll just take the steak dinner, medium, and a Pepsi."

"I like that, a man who knows how to order," the waitress quipped.

Jack couldn't resist firing back: "Well they say the simpler the man, the quicker the order."

After a hearty laugh, she replied, "That's a good one, I'll have to remember that. I'll be right back."

As Jack polished off the excellent steak sometime later, the waitress returned to clear his plate. "All done now?"

"Yes, that was one heck of a steak, thank you," Jack said appreciatively.

"Well, we are close to the source," she hinted.

Jack looked perplexed. "Come again?"

"The beef," she clarified. "It's local."

A light bulb went off in Jack's head. "Say, I wonder if you could answer a question for me?"

"Sure, go ahead," the friendly woman replied.

"Henry Riddell, you ever heard of him?"

She laughed at the coincidence. "Heard of him? That's the damnedest thing, you're eating his beef!"

Jack chuckled in surprise. "Well I'll be, that's one hell of a coincidence!"

"That sure is," the waitress agreed. "What did you want to know?"

Seeing an opportunity, Jack asked casually, "Do you know anything about him?"

"Well, he's pretty well known around these parts," she offered. "He's active in anything that's Sweetwater. You know he won the lottery, right?"

Jack nodded. "I heard that."

"Well, you wouldn't know it," she went on. "He's the same old Henry. As they say, good as the summer days are long."

This intrigued Jack. "I've been looking to get a hold of him."

The waitress eyed him curiously. "He in some kind of trouble?"

"No. Nothing like that, I'm just interviewing lottery winners and he was on my list."

"You some kind of reporter?" she asked, not fully buying it.

Jack hedged just a bit. "You could say that..."

The friendly waitress nodded knowingly. "Well in that case, his farm is down this road about 3 miles. Make a left on Old Mill Road and you can't miss it. It's on your right, there's a big sign that says, 'Riddell Ranch.'"

"That's very helpful, thank you," Jack said gratefully.

"No problem, the pleasure was mine."

A short while later, Jack pulled up to the Riddell Ranch, but didn't see any activity around the main house. He got out and knocked on the front door but there was no answer. Glancing around the sprawling property, he spotted Henry's pickup truck parked about a quarter mile down the road.

Jack drove over and found Henry working on repairing a fence line. He pulled up alongside and called out, "Excuse me, do you know where I could find Henry Riddell?"

The rancher squinted over at him. "You're talking to him. What can I do for you?"

"Good afternoon, Mr. Riddell," Jack said, getting out of the car. "My name is Jack Peterson. I believe I left you a couple messages."

Henry nodded in recognition. "Yeah, I got those. I meant to call...I've been really busy." He extended his hand. "Call me Henry, if you would."

They shook firmly as Jack replied, "Henry it is...Call me Jack. I bet you stay plenty busy with a spread like this."

"Yes sir, there's always something to tend to," Henry said matter-of-factly.

"Do you have a few minutes to talk?" Jack asked.

The rancher considered this while surveying the remaining fence work. "What can I help you with?"

"I wanted to ask you some questions about JTB Investments and Mr. John Smith."

Understanding flickered in Henry's eyes. "JTB, huh? Tell you what, I need to get this tended to by dark. It'd be better if you came back around suppertime, say 7:30?"

Jack quickly agreed. "That would be fine, at the main house?"

"Yes sir," Henry confirmed. "And bring your appetite."

"Well, I wouldn't want to impose," Jack demurred.

But Henry would have none of it. "No sir, I insist. I owe you that for not calling back. It's no problem at all."

Realizing it would be rude to refuse, Jack relented with a smile. "That's mighty nice of you. I haven't had a home cooked meal in a month of Sundays."

"Great, well I better get this finished," Henry said, tipping his hat. "I'll expect you around 7:30 then."

"Okay Henry, I'll let you finish up. See you tonight."

As Jack drove off, Henry watched him go, his eyes narrowed pensively against the setting sun.

At the Sweetwater Inn, Jack was greeted by Grady Tanner, an affable older man who moved with the practiced ease of a lifelong hotelier.

"Need a room?" Grady asked as Jack approached the desk.

"Yes."

"Just you?"

Jack nodded. "Yes, that's it."

"Smoking or non-smoking?" came the standard inquiry.

With a regretful chuckle, Jack replied, "Smoking."

Grady didn't miss a beat. "Well hell, they all been smoked in, I don't know why I ask." He slid the registration card across the counter. "Do me a favor and fill this out if you would."

"No problem." Jack scribbled out his information and handed it back.

"What do I owe you?" he asked, pulling out his wallet.

Grady squinted at the form. "One night?"

"One, maybe two," Jack hedged.

"$43.50 with tax," the old timer calculated. "If you want that second night let me know by 10 tomorrow. We get busy come Thursday."

Jack agreed to those terms. "I'll do that."

"Number 7 is back around that way, you can't miss it." Grady handed him the key as they shook hands.

"And what's your name?" Jack asked.

"Grady...Grady Tanner."

"You here on business?" the old man asked curiously.

Jack confirmed it with a nod. "Yep."

"Well let me know if I can get you anything," Grady offered hospitably.

"Will do, thank you."

As Jack headed for his room, Grady called after him with a chuckle, "Yeah, take 'er easy."

Later that evening, Jack was perusing the local newspaper when a small article caught his eye about a little league baseball team called the Riddell Rangers who were sponsored by none other than Henry Riddell himself. The brief piece praised the undefeated squad and their "generous" patron who had provided equipment, facilities, you name it.

"Yeah, he's a regular Charles Manson," Jack muttered sardonically under his breath.

A while later and exhausted Jack lays napping on the bed. He rustles slightly in a dream state.

Flashback to 1968 in Vietnam.

Lance corporal Jackson "Jack" Peterson and Lance corporal James "Jimmy" Chavez are perched atop ammo cans with their backs against the fighting hole wall. Their heads peak out above as they both stare out unto the horizon with the brilliant streams of light dancing over the sky as the sun goes to bed in Khe Sanh Vietnam. It's very peaceful at this moment. Each man takes a swig off their canteen without uttering a word. They seem completely enthralled in this spectacle of beauty. Just then Jimmy breaks the silence.

"You remember the 54 Chevy I have."

"Yeah, man. I love that car."

"My mom says my uncle is gonna fix it up for me for when we get back. My cousin is getting the body straight and my uncle is gonna paint it"

"Wow, you're lucky. My old man said I could have his Nova when I get back, but I can't be driving a Nova. Now if it was a Camaro, that would be another story. A convertible, black with a black top. Man, the chicks would be all over that."

Jimmy laughs, "You're too damn picky."

"Nah, I appreciate it, but damn… A Nova?"

Jimmy gets reflective.

"I think about that car a lot. And sometimes I wonder if I'm ever gonna drive it again?"

"Stop with that negative crap. You'll drive it… It won't be long. We got 5 months left. Then the long ride home."

Jimmy looks down and picks up a rock and throws it out of the hole.

"I never wanna come back here. This place is death…hell it smells like death."

Jack retorts "Yeah, but this sunset is like it was painted. What's God doing painting this spectacle for all us down here trying to murder each other?"

Jimmy snaps, "Men created this war. I don't think God is anywhere near this place."

"God's everywhere Jimmy, even in this hell hole."

Jimmy laments "It's hard to understand why we had to come 9000 miles to try and avoid being killed."

Jack punches Jimmy in the arm, "You're killing my vibe bro. Lets just sit back and enjoy the sunset. We'll be knee deep in it soon enough."

Knowing how true that statement was, they both smile and stare off into the distance.

Jack wakes up from his nap and abruptly sits up in bed. Rubbing the memories from his eyes he slowly grasps that he's been dreaming of another time and another place.

Chapter Five

~ The Ranch ~

As the sun began to set over Sweetwater, Jack wandered outside and discovers Grady sitting in a chair out front, no doubt enjoying the nightly display with the setting sun.

"Good evening, how's it going?" Jack called out.

"Good evening," the old man replied genially. "Great, take a seat."

Jack didn't need to be asked twice. "I don't mind if I do."

He settled into the chair next to Grady and they watched in companionable silence as vibrant reds, oranges and pinks streaked across the sky. Finally, Jack spoke in a hushed tone of awe, as if observing the phenomenon for the first time.

"Just think, it happens every day and I don't even notice. Probably haven't done this for 30 years. It's so hard just to sit still nowadays."

Grady nodded sagely. "That's a damn shame, sometimes we get so busy in life we forget what's really important, too much stuff in the way."

The words resonated with Jack. "No truer words have been spoken."

"Ah, it ain't just you," Grady said with a wheezy chuckle. "Hell, half the world is on their cell phone or the internet. Pretty soon talking in person will be as uncomfortable as a trip to the dentist."

Jack had to agree. "I hear ya, damn technology is speeding the world too fast."

"That's the truth," the old-timer railed. "Hardly anything is written down anymore, you noticed that? Fax, email, voicemail if you don't have it, people look at you funny. Once the power goes out, we're done for."

"You are sure right about that," Jack murmured somberly.

Grady shook his head. "Shame, I tell you. Damn shame."

As the sun dipped below the horizon in an explosion of fiery reds and oranges, reminiscent of the sunset in Vietnam, the two men paused to take in the heavenly sight, each lost in their own thoughts until Jack finally broke the silence.

"I was reading that your little league team is doing pretty good."

Grady immediately perked up with obvious pride. "Those kids, they can sure play. When they have a game, the whole dang town turns out."

"I read Henry Riddell sponsored that team," Jack mentioned casually.

"Oh, Henry, he's great," Grady effused. "They got fancy new equipment and all sorts of stuff. You ought to see those kids play, their..." He trailed off wistfully. "They love that new field, the pro team should have a field that nice."

Jack probed carefully. "Henry's a special guy, huh?"

Grady grew solemn and nodded slowly. "Well...you know he won the lottery?"

"Yeah, I heard that," Jack confirmed.

"He deserved it," Grady stated firmly. "That's a hardworking man. His whole family has been that way, they've been in Sweetwater forever."

Sensing he was pushing his luck, Jack decided to bow out gracefully for now. "I'd like to sit a little longer, but I've got an appointment." He rose stiffly from the chair. "Nice talking to you..."

But as he turned to go, Grady's parting words stopped him in his tracks. "Say, tell Henry I said hello when you see him."

Jack turned back around, a look of consternation on his face. "Come again?"

Grady seemed puzzled by Jack's reaction. "When you have supper, tell him Grady said 'Hi.'"

Realization dawning, Jack asked carefully, "How'd you know that?"

The old man chuckled knowingly. "Sweetwater ain't that big, mister. Word gets around pretty damn quick."

As comprehension set in, Jack could only nod resignedly. "I guess..."

A short while later, Jack pulled up to the Riddell home, the aroma of a home cooked meal thick in the air. He knocked and Henry soon ushered him inside to the dining room where a feast was laid out.

Over the course of the hearty meal, the two men engaged in idle conversation and pleasantries. Once their plates were cleared, Henry moved to pick up Jack's, but jack waved him off.

"Let me get that..."

"No, you're a guest, I won't have it," Henry insisted stubbornly.

"Thank you," Jack said sincerely as Henry carried the dishes to the kitchen. "That was a great meal."

"I have my moments," the rancher called back modestly. "You got me on a good day."

While Henry tended to the dishes, Jack rose to study the various photos, awards and memorabilia adorning the walls. "Who's this here?" he asked, gesturing to one particular. grainy portrait of a 70 something man in overalls.

"That's my Great, Great Granddaddy," Henry called out from the kitchen. "He staked his claim here about 150 years ago. It was just a shack for the first twenty."

Jack let out an impressed whistle. "150 years, my God that's some history."

Henry emerged from the kitchen, standing proudly beside the old portrait. "It's not common, no sir."

"And the rest?" Jack asked, gesturing to the other framed photographs.

Henry starts to point at different pictures. "Granddaddy, Daddy, and my family," Henry explained, his voice thick with pride.

Jack pointed to a picture of two strapping young men. "Those are the boys you mentioned?"

Henry nodded. "Yes, Henry Jr. and William everyone calls him Lil' Bill, but he ain't little."

Jack had to agree, eyeing the burly young man. "He doesn't look little. Where are they now?"

"They wanted to work here on the farm, but I told them only after 4 years of college," Henry said. "JR has two more years and Billy's got three. They come home on breaks and the whole summer."

It was clear where the sons got their solid work ethic. "I guess with this kind of history it's in their blood?"

Henry raised an eyebrow. "Ranching?"

"Yes."

The older man sighed heavily. "It's tough, it ain't like it used to be. Throw some cows out there and take them to auction every six months...no sir. If you don't have the skills nowadays you could be out of business really quick."

"So, what do they major in?" Jack asked curiously.

"Agriculture mainly," Henry replied, "but I tell them get yourself a good education and you'll thank yourself down the road. Even with all this money I still want them to be successful in whatever they do. I was the first to graduate high school and they will be the first for college."

Jack could hear the paternal pride in his voice. "You must be proud of them."

"I tell you those two are my pride and joy," Henry agreed wholeheartedly. "But sometimes I wish I would have had one girl. They kind of give you a different perspective on life."

The wistful comment struck a chord with Jack. "I hear you."

Reading between the lines, Henry asked carefully, "Your boy...What does he do?"

With a slight grimace, Jack admitted, "He's a painter."

Henry looked confused. "Houses? Cars?"

Jack shook his head. "No, picture type painting."

Understanding dawned on the rancher's face. "He sounds creative."

"He gets that from his mother," Jack said.

Sensing the raw emotions there, Henry tread lightly. "Been married long?"

But Jack didn't mince words. "Separated for some time and she has since passed."

Henry's expression was full of sympathy. "Sorry to hear that, it must be hard on the boy."

Lost in his own regrets, Jack replied hollowly, "I guess, but he never says much."

The older man leveled with him. "Don't take this the wrong way but the hard stuff is up to you."

"You mean about his mother?" Jack asked, not comprehending.

Henry met his gaze steadily. "It's tough knowing what's too much. My rule of thumb is, with your kids, just swallow the pride it goes down easier than failure."

Jack looked away, considering this perspective that was so foreign to him. "I'm not sure it's pride."

But Henry didn't press him further. "Anyway, I think you know what I mean."

After a contemplative pause, Jack nodded slowly. "Yeah...I guess that's one of my problems. I'll keep that in mind."

Sensing they'd plumbed the depths of such personal matters enough for now, Henry steered them back on course. "Let's sit out here on the porch and we can talk business. I'll tell you what you want to know."

Out on the serene ranch porch, the two men lit up cigarettes, Henry insisting on providing Jack's light. Once settled in the rocking chairs, Jack broached the main subject.

"Alright, I guess I'll tell you what I know, and you tell me if that's correct, how's that?"

Henry shrugged agreeably. "That'll work."

"You won the lottery about 8 months ago and soon after that you bought shares in JTB Investments with John Smith?"

The rancher nodded. "Yes sir, I did."

"Have you gotten any return on that?" Jack asked pointedly.

"Not exactly," Henry hedged.

Jack pressed the obvious implication. "I guess that means no?"

But Henry remained vague. "Well, being a rancher, you've got to be patient."

"Here's my dilemma," Jack laid it out. "I've found 3 investors and all three are lottery winners and all three haven't made a dime. That's not very good odds, is it?"

Henry had to concede the point. "Well when you say it like that, yes I guess it sounds pretty bad."

"My other thing is none of you, except my client, are very concerned," Jack went on. "If the original winner was alive, I wouldn't even be here talking to you now."

That seemed to amuse the older man. "Now that would be a damn shame, wouldn't it?"

Laughing it off, he tried to reassure Jack. "Listen, I'm pretty set for life with the money I got left. It's true I made an investment with a large amount of those winnings I won't deny that. But I'm living the dream, how could I complain?"

But Jack wasn't dissuaded so easily. "I've got to get to the bottom of this. It's what I was hired to do."

Henry raised an eyebrow quizzically. "And what will you accomplish?"

It was Jack's turn to shrug. "Well for one, I'll get to the bottom of Mr. Smith. He's definitely not on the up and up. That's for sure."

"Things don't always appear as they really are, Jack," Henry said cryptically. "Can I tell you a story?"

Intrigued despite himself, Jack replied, "By all means."

Henry launched into the rural parable. "There was this man driving down the road and he comes to this farm and in the field is this pig, but on the back end of this pig is a wheelbarrow tied up and no legs. So, the man walks up to the house and knocks on the door."

He continued spinning the yarn at a leisurely pace: "A farmer answers the door and asks what he can do for the man and he says, 'What's the story on that pig?' The farmer says, 'That's one fantastic pig.' The man says, 'How so?' The farmer says, 'One night that pig came up to the house late at night and started banging and snorting on the back door, so I get up to see what the hell is going on.'"

Jack was engrossed as Henry went on. "'I look out back and the barn was on fire, so I go out and get all the livestock out and put out the fire.' The man says, 'That's amazing.' The farmer says, 'Another time that pig came up to the house during the day and practically dragged my wife out into the pasture.' That's when she saw my youngin had fallen into the well and that saved her life.'"

Henry paused for dramatic effect. "The man says, 'That's totally amazing but what happened to its hind legs?' The farmer said proudly, 'Well you don't eat a fantastic pig like that all at once now, do ya?'"

Jack joined Henry in a deep belly laugh at the absurd punchline. "That's a good one!"

"My daddy told me that one, it's got to be old," Henry admitted. "But like I said, things aren't always like they appear."

Jack considered this sagely advice. "Not always."

"Excuse me for a moment," Henry said, rising stiffly from his rocking chair. "I'm going to use the restroom, I'll be right back out."

As the rancher lumbered inside, Jack took the opportunity to pull out his notebook and jot down a few thoughts, his brow furrowed in contemplation of the many seemingly contradictory pieces of this puzzle he was trying to assemble.

Jack took the opportunity to jot down some notes about their conversation. A few minutes later, he heard the rancher's heavy footsteps approaching.

"Jack, let me show you the barn," Henry called out.

"Alright," Jack agreed, rising and following him outside.

As they strolled across the property, Henry asked ponderously, "Jack, is there a point where you say, 'That's all there is'?"

Jack considered the philosophical question. "I guess, I guess in everything there's that point. I was hired to do a job and I take that seriously."

But Henry seemed resigned. "Sometimes you just got to accept things for what they are."

"That's only if you know what they are, Henry," Jack countered carefully. "If you're mixed up in something it would be a good idea to get it out now."

The rancher shook his head. "I wish there was something I could say, but I really don't have anything."

They arrived at the enormous barn, its weathered doors standing ajar. "This is a huge barn," Jack remarked.

"Yes sir, it's a big one," Henry agreed. "But with anything this size you've got lots of varmints in it."

Jack looked around cautiously. "Like what?"

"Rats and such..." As if on cue, Henry reached into his jacket pocket and pulled out a revolver while Jack's back was turned.

Just then Jack caught a sight of the gun and the hairs on the back of Jack's neck prick up and he turned. "What's going on, Hen…"

But before he could finish, the rancher raised the gun skyward and fired a deafening shot straight up into the air. Jack flinched, his heart pounding as his hand instinctively went for his own weapon tucked into his waistband.

"Jesus Christ, Henry, you scared the crap out of me!" Jack yelled over the ringing in his ears.

"Sorry, it's best to catch them off guard," Henry said with an unsettling smile, gesturing to the sudden stream of bats pouring out of the upper loft, screeching and flapping wildly away from the disturbance.

Jack's blood was still racing as he processed what had just happened. "Bats, make a damn mess," the rancher said calmly, almost to himself.

"I guess it is..." Jack managed to gulp out, furious at himself for being so easily spooked.

Henry seemed to pick up on his rattled state. "Is there anymore you want to know about what we talked about?"

Struggling to regain his composure, Jack shook his head slowly. "No, I think I've got it. But do me a favor and tell Mr. Smith I am looking to talk to him. You can give him this number."

He handed Henry his business card, which the rancher pocketed. "Sure thing."

"I appreciate that..."

Henry clapped him on the shoulder in a gesture of finality. "Well then I best be getting to my nightly chores."

"I've got to get going myself," Jack said quickly, eager to put some distance between them.

"Let me know if you need anything else," Henry offered.

Jack shook his hand again, firmly this time. "Thanks for dinner, it was great."

As he walked briskly back to his car, Jack could still feel his heart pounding from the adrenaline spike. He wrenched open the glove compartment and pulled out his revolver, checking the cylinder before shoving it back into his waistband with shaky hands.

"Son of a bench..." he muttered under his breath, pulling out onto the dirt road perhaps a bit faster than was wise.

Back at the Sweetwater Inn that night, Jack sat numbly in his room, staring sightlessly at the wall as he replayed the unnerving encounter at the Riddell Ranch. Removing his glasses, he rubbed his tired eyes wearily before his gaze fell on the newspaper story about the little league team again. An idea seemed to form, and he suddenly grabbed his cell phone, dialing a number he knew by heart.

"Jack, is that you?" came Kathy's voice.

"It's not too late, is it?" Jack asked hesitantly.

"No, I'm a night owl," she reassured him. "It's tough for me to go to bed early these days."

Jack took that in with a nod, forging ahead. "I visited with Henry Riddell tonight."

"Any news?" Kathy asked expectantly.

But Jack deflated. "No, the same old story. No problem with him and he seems to be on the up and up."

"Alright, what's next?" she pressed.

Jack sighed heavily. "That's what I'm calling about, I'm not sure if we have anything to go on."

There was a disappointed pause before Kathy said, "So that's it, huh?"

"Well, that's what it seems like," Jack admitted reluctantly. "I don't want to let you down but I'm really getting nowhere."

To his surprise, Kathy didn't sound discouraged. "You've done a great job, Jack. If you think that's the end, then I'll accept that."

Still, Jack felt compelled to explain further. "I hate to leave this unfinished but for right now, I'm at a dead end."

"Jack, I know you've done your best," Kathy said kindly. "Don't fret now."

Emboldened by her understanding, Jack offered, "Let me think on it and I'll talk to you tomorrow."

"Okay, give me a call," she agreed. "And Jack...you get some rest."

"I will. Good night."

The next morning, Jack was roused from a fitful sleep by the jarring ring of his cell phone. He groped groggily for the source of the noise, fumbling with the alarm clock before realizing it was his phone.

"Jack here..." he mumbled into the receiver, squinting against the sunlight streaming in.

"Mr. Peterson?" came an English accented voice on the other end.

Jack sat up straighter in the bed, suddenly fully awake. "This is Jack Peterson, who's calling?"

"Good morning, Mr. Peterson," the smooth voice replied. "This is John Smith. I hear you've been looking to talk to me."

For a long moment, Jack could only stammer incoherently as he processed this unexpected turn of events, quickly rising from the bed. "Yes...um yes I have," he finally managed.

Struggling to gather his wits, Jack paced the room and slipped on his glasses as Mr. Smith continued, "You're a tough man to find, it seems."

"Yes, I suppose I'm always on the go," the elusive man replied easily.

Jack decided to seize the moment. "Where are you now, Mr. Smith?"

"I'm on the road going back to the office," came the unhurried reply.

Here was his chance. "I'd like to ask you a few questions, if I could?"

There was a noticeably long pause before Smith answered, "How about we talk face to face? Could you meet me there?"

Relief washed over Jack. "Sure," he said without hesitation.

"Alright then, I'll be in my office Friday noon. Is that soon enough?"

"Yes, that will be great," Jack confirmed, scribbling down the details.

"You have my number now," Smith stated. "Let me know if that's going to be a problem."

"Okay, I'll do that."

A long pause and then Mr. Smith responds, "Mr. Peterson, is there anything else?"

Jack considered pressing for more but decided to bide his time for now. "No, I guess we'll talk Friday."

"Then I'll see you then. Good day."

"See you then, thank you," Jack said, still flustered as he hung up the phone. He stood there for a long moment, processing what had just happened before muttering under his breath, "Damn it..."

It was time to ante up and finally get some real answers from the mysterious John Smith himself. Jack just hoped he was ready for whatever truth awaited him at the end of this twisted trail.

Chapter Six

~ Jimmy ~

Later in the early morning, Jack stopped by the front desk to settle his bill and check out of the Sweetwater Inn. Grady was working his usual shift.

"Checking out?" the old-timer asked as Jack approached.

"Yep, all done," Jack confirmed with a tight smile.

Grady raised an eyebrow shrewdly. "Did you tell Henry I said hello?"

Grimacing, Jack admitted, "You know I forgot all about that, sorry."

"No problem. Did he tell you the whole story about losing the farm and such?"

Jack looked puzzled. "Losing the farm?"

Grady nodded gravely. "He's so modest, that man. Well two days before he won, he was on his way to file for bankruptcy. The papers were all drawn up and everything. Isn't that the damnedest thing?"

Realization began to dawn on Jack's face. "So that's how he saved that farm?"

"I thought you were writing the story?"

"Well check on it over at the newspaper," Grady advised, "and they ought to have the whole scoop. It's good stuff."

Intrigued despite himself, Jack made a note of it. "Thanks, I'll have to do that."

"Not a problem," Grady said cheerfully. "It's a great story."

As Jack signed his checkout receipt, he couldn't help but mutter sarcastically under his breath, "Yeah, it just keeps getting better."

A short while later found Jack hunched over an old microfiche reader at The Sweetwater Reporter's offices, squinting at the tiny print until he located the article he wanted. Leaning back, he read the headline out loud to himself:

"Local Rancher Hits It Big Henry Riddell hit more than the lottery, he saved a Texas institution from going under. For almost 150 years, Riddell Ranch has been one of Texas's longest running working ranches. On Monday, Henry Riddell was all set to put an end to this and file for bankruptcy, but winning the lottery not only saved the farm but a way of life..."

Jack shook his head in disbelief as he continued reading: "Henry attributes his winning to clean living, good luck and prayer. As many say, it couldn't have happened to a better man. Congratulations Henry!"

"You've got to be kidding me," Jack muttered under his breath. This was getting more unbelievable by the minute.

Later, Jack found himself at a dusty rural crossroads a few miles outside of Sweetwater, sitting in his idling car as he stared down each empty road stretching out before him. His brow was furrowed in indecision as he looked from left to right and back again, seemingly awaiting some cosmic sign to point him in the right direction.

Finally, in utter frustration, Jack cried out to no one, "Which way to go, come on?"

But the windswept silence provided no answers. With a heavy sigh, Jack put the car into drive and eased out onto the desolate road only to be immediately confronted by another vehicle approaching the intersection.

As the other car slowed to a stop, Jack glanced over to see a kindly elderly nun smiling at him from behind the wheel. Without a word, she gestured to her right with a gentle nod, as if indicating the proper path.

Jack couldn't help but return the knowing smile as clarity washed over him. Everything was beginning to make sense, however improbable it seemed. He nodded his thanks to the wise sister and turned his car onto the road she had indicated a road that ultimately led him back to Nogales and the St. John Vianney Orphanage.

It was evening when Jack arrived. Peering through the window, he could see the office appeared closed up for the night, but a light burned steadily in Father Diaz's private quarters.

Jack rapped lightly on the door, half-expecting no answer at this late hour. But the priest's muffled voice soon called out, "Who's there?"

"Jack Peterson, Father," he replied, hoping he wasn't disturbing the man's evening too much.

"Come in," Father Diaz invited without a hint of impatience.

Jack entered cautiously to find the priest undoing his collar and leaning back in his chair, the very picture of serenity. "I'm sorry it's late, I needed to ask you a couple more questions if I could?"

"Well yes, I was just finishing up," Father Diaz said easily. "You caught me at a great time."

As Jack took a seat across from him, he began feeling uncharacteristically awkward. "I know this might seem kind of strange..."

But the priest just smiled disarmingly. "No... Not at all, I'm more than happy to help."

Still, Jack couldn't shake his hesitation, studying Father Diaz's open expression intently as the older man regarded him with concern.

"Is there something wrong, Mr. Peterson? You look troubled."

Jack exhaled heavily. "It's a lot of things..." He paused, searching for the right words. "Did you happen to hear from Mr. Smith and give him my number?"

"No," Father Diaz replied easily. "Why do you ask? Have you heard from him recently?"

Nodding slowly, Jack confirmed, "Yes, I'm meeting him in his office Friday. But something still doesn't seem right."

The priest looked momentarily taken aback. "Well, I thought that was what you wanted, Mr. Peterson?"

"Yeah, me too," Jack admitted heavily. "But I suppose it's gotten more complicated than that."

Father Diaz leaned forward intently. "How so?"

Meeting the other man's sincere gaze, Jack laid it out there. "It's everything...Tell me something, Father. Were you in some kind of trouble before you won that lottery?"

The blunt question seemed to catch Father Diaz off-guard. "What do you mean?"

"I mean, were you in dire straits of some sorts?" Jack pressed carefully.

The question clearly made the priest uncomfortable, but he considered it seriously before responding carefully, "That's an odd question..."

As Father Diaz studied him intently, Jack could see the internal wheels turning, debating how much to reveal. Finally, the older man sighed and replied, "I guess you could say it came at a very fortunate time."

Jack gave a slow nod, pieces clicking into place. In a near whisper, he said, "Would you say it was, pardon the expression..."a godsend?'"

A look of amazement flickered across Father Diaz's face before he let out a rusty chuckle. "Hmm...that sounds like you're thinking spiritually now?"

Father Diaz features turned contemplative as he mulled over Jack's provocative wording. "But yes...I guess you could say that. It was a godsend."

Gently but insistently, Jack pressed, "Tell me about that, if you would."

Father Diaz tilted his head inquisitively, as if still in disbelief at the strange turn their conversation had taken. But he acquiesced readily enough.

"Well, the orphanage had lost most of its funding and the donations were getting very thin," he began, sorrow lining his weathered face. "Everything costs money and we had little of it. The Cardinal called me to inform me that under the circumstances, we would be forced to close our doors in less than eight weeks."

He paused; the pain of the memory still clearly raw. "I was sick with guilt that I had not done enough to save this place. We all prayed for a miracle. Then, like a sign from above, I hit that lottery and like that, all that was needed was provided. The Church considered it a blessing and made keeping this place open a top priority."

A glimmer of pride shone through as the priest added, "Also, consider I donated 50% of my winnings to them. That alone was enough to get into their good graces."

Jack slowly shook his head in disbelief, pieces continuing to fall into place. When he finally spoke, his voice was hushed with awe. "I think you knew you'd win."

The simple statement hung in the air as Father Diaz just smiled serenely. After an endless moment, Jack looked down at his hands, unable to meet the other man's knowing gaze.

"Is there anything else?" the priest prompted gently.

Jack struggled to put his swirling thoughts and emotions into words. "For one, I think I'm involved in something far beyond my comprehension, Father. I know that for a fact..." He trailed off before continuing seriously, "I don't know exactly what you're all up to, but you're up to something, that I'm sure of."

"I assure you, Mr. Peterson, I'm not up to anything," Father Diaz said evenly, holding his gaze.

But Jack wasn't dissuaded. "You may not be up to anything illegal, but I don't know it all, is my point."

The priest considered this carefully before replying, "It seems to me that you got what you came looking for, Mr. Peterson."

Jack quipped, "Maybe that's the point."

After a brief silence Father Diaz said gently. "Try having a little faith."

Jack looked taken aback. "Faith?"

His gaze was drawn to the crucifix hanging on the wall, the haunting image of the suffering Christ. Studying it intently, he said in a low voice, "Faith hasn't always served me all that well, Father. It has been a long time since I relied on faith."

The priest regarded him with compassionate understanding. "Can I venture a guess? I suspect you lost your faith during a time of struggle. Where that was, I have no idea and maybe that isn't even important. But you must try and find your way back. With its absence, we are left with emptiness." He paused before adding solemnly, "My advice is to believe in something, Mr. Peterson. He'll help you find the light inside the dark."

Seeing Jack's pensive expression, Father Diaz backtracked slightly. "Sorry, I didn't mean to give you a sermon, just an observation."

But Jack rebuffed the apology. "Don't be sorry, it's just...it's just not me."

Jack rose from his chair, still visibly grappling with the spiritual implications the priest had raised.

Jack slightly unsettled. "I appreciate the time and I'll think about what we've discussed."

Jack extended his hand and Father Diaz stood to shake it firmly. Father Diaz stated warmly "It was my pleasure. I think you're on the right track."

As they made their way to the front door, Jack stopped with one final question. "One more thing, kind of on that previous subject..."

"Yes?" the priest prompted.

"Do you think God hears all our prayers?" Jack asked hesitantly. "I mean, do you believe that's possible? With billions of people needing his help every day, it just never seemed possible to me."

Father Diaz considered the profound query carefully before responding, "A good question, I have been asked that before. My answer usually is God hears all of us. But, I am leaning towards, I believe all our prayers are heard."

Jack mulled that over. "So, you think they're not wasted?"

"My son," the priest said kindly, placing a hand on Jack's shoulder. "They're never wasted. When we pray, we demonstrate our belief."

As Jack processed this platitude, a melancholy look came over his face. "I think I know what you mean."

On the long drive from Nogales to Kingman, Jack's mind wanders back over 30 years to day that had challenged his faith in humanity to its core.

It was mid-February 1968, and the battalion was hunkered down at the bitterly contested Khe Sanh combat base in Vietnam. As the sun began to set in an amber glow, Jack and Jimmy sat watching in silence from their sandbagged fighting hole.

"You ever get homesick?" Jimmy asked Jack wistfully, his feet propped up against the opposite wall.

Jack shrugged, fiddling absently with his rosary beads. "I guess I'm more sick of this crap than homesick."

Jimmy stared out at the rising plumes of smoke over the devastated jungle landscape. "At least it's quiet today. Maybe it's all over?"

But Jack knew better, having endured weeks of the unrelenting shelling and ground assaults.

Jack replies, "I doubt that, how long have we been in this? It's gotta be three weeks at least?"

"Damn, three weeks," Jimmy mused with a mirthless chuckle. "That's crazy."

Gripping the worn crucifix, Jack raised it to his lips and planted an eager kiss on the metallic image. "Protect us another day," he whispered fervently.

Jimmy eyed the rosary enviously. "That's been good luck. I have to get mine blessed by the chaplain tomorrow. My mom sent it last mail call."

Jack looked up sharply. "Tomorrow?"

"Yeah, tomorrow," Jimmy confirmed casually. "It's Ash Wednesday...the start of Lent. Oh, and it's Valentines Day if you've got a sweetheart." Jimmy laughs.

Jack gives him a sly grin. "Only you sweet cheeks."

Jimmy shoots him an annoyed stare. "Man, being in this place, I've almost forgotten what girls are."

"It won't be long, we'll get R & R in a month. Then you can get reacquainted." Jack gives him a wink

Realization flickered in Jack's eyes as the ubiquitous passage of time became starkly apparent. "Ash Wednesday is tomorrow?

"Dang, I totally lost track of time." He gestured for Jimmy to hand over the religious article. "Let me see the rosary."

But Jimmy relented. "I don't have it on, man, I got it stuffed right here in my pocket. Nobody can touch it yet. I told you, I need to get it blessed."

"I'd put it on anyway," Jack urged gravely. "We need all the help we can get."

The two Marines lapsed into silence once more, each instinctively knowing it would not last. Finally, Jimmy sat up straighter and mimed holding an imaginary serving tray.

"Feel like some delicious dinner Monsieur?" he asked in a hokey French butler's accent. "Since it's my turn, what would you like today, sir?"

Jack rolled his eyes good-naturedly. "Very funny..."

Jimmy grinned. "I'll tell you what, let's make it a surprise."

"What surprise?" Jack groused. "We're having lousy C-Rats again for the hundredth consecutive day. And tomorrow we'll have C-Rats again."

But Jimmy refused to be deterred from his playful banter. "Hey man, you never know."

Jack snorted sarcastically. "Yeah, maybe we'll have a juicy steak."

Jimmy's grin widened as he fired back without missing a beat. "How do you want yours done?"

Deciding to play along, Jack pretended to consider it. "I don't care, just some real meat. That would be like heaven."

Chuckling, Jimmy sprang lightly to his feet. "Alright devil dog, I'll be right back..."

He jogged off in a crouched run but turned back just before rounding the corner out of sight. With a jaunty wink and wave, Jimmy's smiling face was suddenly frozen in Jack's memory the last peaceful image before all hell broke loose.

Some indeterminable time later, it could have been a half hour or just minutes, Jack was jolted by the deafening barrage of explosions rocking the earth itself. Bombs, gunfire, and mortars were dropping all around inside the perimeter, shrieks of agonizing death and cries for "corpsmen" rising up from every direction.

"Jimmy!" Jack bellowed into the fiery maelstrom; his voice drowned out by the cacophony of chaos. He didn't know where Jimmy was, only that his friend had not returned.

Jack is up in the prone position with his M16 loaded with a round in the chamber. Jack is amped up waiting to take a shot as soon as he can see even the enemy, but the smoke and dust is making seeing anything impossible.

Then through the smoke, Jack spotted Jimmy, lying motionless about 15 yards away. Jack sprints through the rain of shrapnel and dirt, flinging himself near Jimmy and crawling to drag Jimmy back towards fighting hole by the shoulders. All Jack could see was blood...a gaping exit wound on Jimmy's left side spewed forth a river of crimson onto the earthen floor.

Jack ripped off his cartridge belt and cinched it around the injury, pulling out first aid supplies and shoving gauze into the area and applying as much pressure as he could muster. Jimmy's eyes fluttered open, his face ashen. Sucking in a ragged breath, his lips moved almost imperceptibly.

Jack leaned in close, cradling his friend's head off the hard ground. "What is it, Jimmy? I can't hear you!"

Bloody spittle flecked Jimmy's lips as he struggled to speak, his words barely audible. "Jack...don't let them leave me here..."

"I won't, we're gonna get you outta here, Jim," Jack assured him fiercely, blinking away the hot tears that threatened to spill down his begrimed cheeks. "You're gonna be alright."

But Jimmy seemed to gain a final clarity, clutching Jack's sleeve with a weak but insistent grip. "I don't mean that...don't let them leave my body here. Send me back to my mom." A long pause from Jimmy. "You were always a terrible liar, Jackie."

"Don't say that," Jack growled, stubbornly shaking his head in denial. "You hold on, Jim."

Jimmy's face was suddenly peaceful, the ghost of a smile playing on his bloodied lips. "Everything's gonna be okay, Jack. I'm not scared anymore." The carnage continues to reign down.

"Stop talking like that and hold on!" Jack pleaded, desperation creeping into his voice. Jimmy screams "Corpsman!"

But Jimmy seemed to drift further away with each labored breath. "Say a prayer with me, Jackie," he gasped out. "Let's see if that thing has any magic left in it."

With a trembling hand, Jack withdrew the crucifix and rosary from under his flak jacket. Jimmy's fingers closed shakily around Jack's, intertwining, and staining the rosary crimson red as they clutched the sacred object. And there, amidst the storm of death and damnation swirling around them, the two young Marines began to pray zealously, lips moving in silent supplication.

When Jack's eyes finally opened, the explosions had ceased as abruptly as they began. An eerie stillness blanketed the decimated base as tendrils of smoke drifted on the still air. Marine's hurried about tending the wounded.

"Lance Corporal, what's his condition?" came an urgent voice from behind him.

Jack just stared vacantly ahead, still holding Jimmy's lifeless form cradled in his arms. He had felt the precious life sccp out of his friend as they prayed together, their pleas unheeded.

"Marine, what's his condition?!" the voice repeated, more insistently this time.

Slowly, as if emerging from a trance, Jack raised his hollow gaze to the corpsmen standing over the fighting hole.

"He's gone..."

With silent efficiency, one of the men hopped down into the hole, preparing to remove the body. But Jack stopped him with a shout.

"Wait a second!"

He gently laid Jimmy's head on the blood soaked earth and bent to remove the rosary, working it free of his friend's stiffening grasp.

Jack then lifted Jimmy's lolling head and slipped his beads over him reverently, letting the crucifix come to rest on his silent chest.

After a moment's hesitation, Jack looked up at the watching corpsmen imploringly. "You're sending him home, right?"

"I promised him he'd get home." His voice broke as he whispered roughly, "Tell me at least they won't leave him here."

The corpsman's expression was somber but reassuring. "He's going home, bro. We'll make sure of that." He gestured to his assistant. "Come on, help us get him ready for his ride."

With utmost care and tenderness, the three of them extricated Jimmy's broken form from the foxhole, straightening his limbs and laying him reverently on the waiting stretcher. Before they could lift him up, Jack stopped them once more.

Gently removing Jimmy's helmet, Jack placed it over his own heart, cradling it for a long moment. Then he leaned down and touched his friend's pale forehead and with his thumb he made the sign of the cross, a final farewell and benediction.

As Jack watched the solemn procession carry Jimmy away, he clutched the bloodied helmet to his chest as if it were the only thing anchoring him to the world.

Jimmy's forgotten rosary lay abandoned in the carnage-strewn fighting hole, blood soaked bandages and gauze already being carried away on the winds.

<u>Chapter Seven</u>

~ Fate ~

Jack blinked, visibly shaking off the visceral memory as he pulled up outside John Smith's office in downtown Kingman. He took a deep, steadying breath before checking that his revolver was loaded and secured in its holster. Time to finally get some answers.

The bell jangled discordantly as Jack pushed through the front door into the small, spartan office. A distinguished looking gentleman in a crisp suit glanced up from behind the desk, regarding Jack with mild interest over the top of his newspaper.

"Mr. Peterson, is it?" the man said, his voice carrying hints of an English accent.

Jack approached warily, returning the assessing look. "Yes, so we finally meet."

John Smith rose smoothly and extended his hand. "Please, have a seat Mr. Peterson."

As they shook hands, Jack couldn't resist a sarcastic quip. "I hear you've been looking for me."

But the dapper businessman didn't rise to the bait, guiding Jack to one of the chairs before resuming his own seat. "I assume you are puzzled by the whole chain of events?"

Jack stared at John Smith, trying to make sense of everything. "I can't make heads or tails of you or, for that matter, the rest of the people. There's obviously more going on than I know. They seemed unwilling to elaborate. But for some strange reason, I think you're going to tell me."

Smith regarded him evenly. "Why do you say that?"

"Well for one, you're here and you don't come across like you're worried about any of this," Jack pointed out.

The dapper Englishman inclined his head slightly. "I guess you want answers?"

Jack nodded slowly. "I just want to know why I'm here talking to you now. I get the feeling we were bound to meet this day."

"You mean fate," Smith stated.

"Yes, fate or something like it."

Smith was silent for a moment before replying, "So ask me what you want to know."

Leaning forward, Jack cut right to the chase. "The lottery winners...did you provide them with the numbers?"

"The numbers came from me, I won't deny that" Smith admitted frankly.

Jack's brow furrowed. "What is it, some scam? Do you have someone on the inside, what's the angle?"

But Smith shook his head calmly. "No, I don't do anything illegal." He paused before adding, "This might sound odd, but could I start with a little about me?"

Intrigued despite himself, Jack acquiesced. "By all means."

He leaned back in his chair, arms folded across his chest as John Smith began to speak in his cultured British lilt.

"I guess you would need to know about it from the start. I was born in Liverpool in 1940, my family was close-knit and very bluc collar. When I was 14, my father was let go at the mill he worked at for 12 years. We went through hard times after that. My father started to drink because he couldn't face the world without being able to provide for his family. What little money he made he gambled away. He became a very different person."

Smith's voice took on a somber tone as he continued. "One night while I lay down to sleep, I rested my arm on my sister Elizabeth.

"I could feel the caverns that her ribs made under her nightshirt. She was not well. That night I prayed. I prayed that God would find a way to help us out of this utter despair and if he would save my sister, I would serve him well."

He paused, seeming to relive the poignant memory.

"That night I heard two words: 'Destination Unknown.' I didn't know what it meant when I woke, but there on the table was a racing form and my father was preparing to place a wager. I scanned the page and there it was, 'Destination Unknown, listed at 60-1' in the fifth race. I told my father about what had happened to me. I remember he cried and said, "my dear boy, I believe our prayers are answered." Then he set out to muster all the money he could get together, much of it borrowed, and went silently to the racetrack. I had no doubt he would win and neither did he."

A faint smile played across Smith's lips. "With the winnings, he opened up a woodworking shop and made furniture for people who couldn't afford anything expensive. My sister received medical attention and she still lives two blocks from where we were born. My father died some years later, but he never told anyone of what happened and neither did I... well, until today."

Jack stared at him, stunned. "You're talking about your prayers being answered?"

Smith met his gaze steadily. "Yes I am."

But Jack wasn't ready to buy into such supernatural claims so easily. "It's a great story, but forgive me, it's very hard to believe."

The Englishman's expression was patient, almost pitying. "That's where you need faith."

Jack looked taken aback. "Faith?"

"Do you have faith, Mr. Peterson?" Smith asked gently.

Scoffing, Jack shook his head. "Faith in God?"

Smith held his gaze as he reiterated, "Yes, in God...in anything?"

Jack considered this for a long moment before admitting heavily, "I don't know, so I guess the answer would be no."

"But you pray?" Smith probed carefully.

With a reluctant nod, Jack confirmed, "Yes, I've prayed before."

Leaning back, Smith seemed to search Jack's face before revealing, "Let me tell you something I've never told anyone else. My blessing and my curse is that from that day on, I hear the prayers of the desperate and the forgotten."

"They come to me at night like lost children looking for comfort. I embrace them and they open themselves up and I am swallowed whole." He paused, letting the weight of his words sink in. "Soon after that, I receive my instructions, imprinted on my brain and in my heart. I then must seek them out and I soothe their sorrow."

Jack stared at him, trying to process this outlandish claim. Finally, he said slowly, "If all that's true, everybody can't win the lottery, or you'd be caught for sure. If that's the truth, that would explain the companies, wouldn't it?"

A ghost of a smile played across Smith's lips. "You're a step ahead of me."

The pieces were finally falling into place for Jack. "That's why the money just disappears. That's why they hand it over, they never intended to get it back. It's just a funnel for the money. It's like legal money laundering."

Smith inclined his head. "Well, I think you're on to something."

"So, what happens to the money?" Jack pressed.

"As you know, there is suffering all over this world,"

Smith replied evenly. "I think you already have some idea what it's used for. I believe you've done your homework."

Jack considered this, then asked pointedly, "So why didn't you just tell Kathy this story? You could have cut out the whole investigation."

"Kathy is quite aware of all this," Smith stated matter-of-factly.

Jack did a double take. "Come again?"

"Kathy Burns is quite aware of this," the Englishman reiterated calmly. "I had Kathy send for you."

The implication hit Jack like a ton of bricks, and he surged to his feet, agitated and confused. "This was all a game? What the hell is going on! Then why all the cloak and dagger, why all the secrecy? Why not simply tell me what's going on from the start?" He paused, chest heaving as he wrestled with the deception. "Why am I here?"

Smith regarded him levelly. "I asked you before if you prayed. What do you pray for, Mr. Peterson? What promises do you make at night and how far are you willing to go?"

Jack shook his head vehemently. "I've been praying and God's not going to listen to me. A man like me, I don't think so."

"Why do you say that?" Smith asked gently.

With a sad shrug, Jack said simply, "Because like someone's already told me, I've lost my faith."

But Smith pushed back. "Mr. Peterson, if you lost your faith, well you wouldn't be praying now then, would you?"

Jack stands stoically as he absorbed the truth of the statement. After a heavy pause, he relented, "What the hell do you want from me? You want to know what I pray for? Okay..." He sank back into the chair, looking and sounding utterly defeated. "I pray that my son can live another day. I pray that I could just do one thing for him in my miserable life. I pray that if there is a God, help him...help him for me."

Smith's brow creased with concern. "He is ill?"

Jack nodded heavily, emotion clogging his throat. "He's not well, because he has a heart condition. He needs surgery, but he has no insurance. Basically, he's last on the list." He looked up at Smith with naked despair in his eyes.

Jack lamented, "I feel hopeless because I can't help him financially...or emotionally."

"The operation is expensive?" Smith surmised gently.

"Two hundred thousand in coverage or cash," Jack confirmed tonelessly. "You have to be able to afford medical care for 5 years or it's not going to happen. It's hard to believe, isn't it? In this day and age."

Smith was silent for a long moment before asking again, "I ask again, what did you promise in those prayers?"

Jack sighed heavily. "I promised to make something out of my life, to do some good. To stop drinking and gambling, so I can save my son!"

The Englishman cocked his head inquisitively. "And have you been able to do those things?"

With a rueful snort of laughter, Jack replied, "Put it this way, I haven't placed a bet in years. The two others I'm still working on."

Smith held his gaze for a long beat before asking solemnly, "So can I be of service to you, Mr. Peterson?"

Jack studied the older man intensely, gears turning in his mind as he processed everything. Finally, he rose and walked over to the window, staring out at the dusty street unseeingly for a long while.

When Jack finally spoke, his voice was hushed with pensive contemplation.

"Be of service?"

Smith nodded. "Yes."

But Jack shook his head slowly as if waking from a dream. "Maybe accepting this offer seals my fate. If I decide to do what you're suggesting, I gamble and maybe I lose. Besides...how do I know this isn't just part of the game?"

To his surprise, Smith didn't attempt to persuade him further. "I see," he said simply. "That's why you were a tough one. I knew this all along and that's why I couldn't approach you. That's why I had to have you use your own determination to discover the truth or you'd never believe it." He held Jack's gaze steadily. "You're right, I can't help you, Mr. Peterson. You're the only one who can do that now."

Jack absorbed this, feeling strangely adrift. "So that's it?"

Smith gave a slow nod of finality. "The thing you seek is very close. It's something you've searched for most of your life. You have the answers, Mr. Peterson." He paused, letting the weight of his words sink in before adding softly, "Now just find out what the question is."

It felt like the ground had fallen away beneath Jack's feet as the full implications washed over him. "There never was a case...It was all to get me here...all to get me to find you and whatever this all is? So, this is the end of it?"

But John Smith shook his head. "The end for me? Yes. The end for you? No. For you, I believe this is just the beginning."

Jack could only stare at him blankly, struggling to process it all. "Beginning?"

"Clear your mind and it will come to you," Smith said with an inscrutable smile. "Just remember what you've learned so far and you'll find the answer...but there's not much time."

Agitated, Jack turned and began pacing, running a hand through his thinning hair. "I don't really know what's going on anymore."

He turned back to face Smith, eyes pleading for some semblance of clarity. "That's it, I'm on my own?"

The Englishman held his gaze steadily. "You were never on your own, Mr. Peterson. None of us are. But you must please hurry." His voice took on an urgency that sent a shiver down Jack's spine. "You need to be back in California before 7 PM tomorrow...that's when the draw is made."

The cryptic statement hung in the air as Jack struggled to process the onslaught of revelations and seeming contradictions. He opened his mouth to respond but no words came, his mind racing as he tried in vain to make sense of it all.

Jack stared at John Smith, utterly at a loss. "I better get going then..." He shook his head slowly. "But where is the real question?"

Smith rose and extended his hand. "Good luck."

Jack grasped it numbly. "Yeah, I think I'll need it."

He turned and walked out of the small office, his mind whirling with doubts and uncertainties over what his next move should be.

That night found Jack driving aimlessly down a deserted highway, the inky blackness illuminated only by the dim glow of his headlights. His voice rumbled in the quiet cabin as he spoke his troubled thoughts aloud.

"Making a promise isn't a tough thing. Keeping it is the tough part." He sighed heavily. "What does happen to all those prayers that are made, the ones that don't find a place to rest? Are they still out there waiting to be heard? Are they floating out there somewhere like a leaf in the wind?"

Up ahead, Jack spotted a dirt access road and pulled off abruptly, slamming on the brakes and killing the engine. He got out and popped the trunk, staring down at the bottle of whiskey he had purchased what seemed like an eternity ago. After a moment's hesitation, he snatched it up and got back behind the wheel, the brown paper bag crinkling in his white-knuckled grip.

Bracing the bottle between his knees, Jack tore off the top of the bag and slowly unscrewed the cap, holding it to his nose and inhaling the harsh fumes. Tears welled up unbidden in his reddened eyes as a lifetime of inner demons clawed their way to the surface. With a ragged sob, he upended the bottle and took a long pull, the fiery liquid searing its way into his mouth.

But at the last second, Jack's self-preservation instincts kicked in and he turned his head, spewing the whiskey out the window in a frothy stream. He hurled the bottle away in disgust, the glass shattering against the side of the road.

Jack then collapsed forward over the steering wheel, shoulders shaking with racking sobs of equal parts anguish and relief at having resisted temptation, if only for the moment.

In a hazy dream, Jack was suddenly transported back to another cemetery on another sun-drenched day years earlier. He and his son Shawn, then around 20 years old, stood beside Margaret's freshly dug grave, bouquets of flowers in hand. Even at that tender age, bitterness and anger radiated off the younger man in waves.

Stomping up to the headstone, Shawn whirled around to confront his father, eyes blazing. "Why did you even come here?"

Jack was taken aback. "What?"

"Why would you come to visit someone you didn't even get along with?" Shawn spat out contemptuously.

Stung, Jack tried to get a handle on his son's outburst. "Where's this coming from?"

But Shawn was on a roll, unleashing years of pent-up resentment. "I mean it's so phony, it's like you're doing it all for show!"

"I loved your mother, you know that" Jack stated simply, unable to muster any anger in response.

Shawn's scathing tone said otherwise. "You did? Well then why didn't you come around while she was sick?"

"She didn't want me around, Shawn..." Jack said wearily, as if they had been through this a thousand times before.

"That was your excuse to stay away," Shawn shot back. "She didn't want your pity!"

Jack ran a hand over his face, realizing there would be no placating his son today. "Do we have to do this now?"

"You tell me when you're ready," Shawn snarled, turning on his heel and stalking away towards the grave marker.

But Jack called after him desperately, "You don't know how close we were! And I don't have to take that tone from you!"

Stopping in his tracks, Shawn slowly pivoted back, a look of pure venom on his young face. "What are you going to do, kick my ass? Go ahead, I don't care anymore!"

At his wit's end, Jack threw up his hands helplessly. "Jesus Christ, am I cursed or what? Can I get a break?"

Closing the distance between them, Shawn loomed over his father tauntingly. "Why, because it's the truth? You never cared; you were too busy!"

Reflexively dismissive, Jack responded with sarcasm. "Forgive me for making a living."

But Shawn wouldn't back down, his next words cutting Jack to his core: "Yeah...It was a living...But it wasn't a life."

The memory abruptly dissipated as Jack jolted awake, his cheek stuck to the seat by dried tears and drool. He sits up. Blinking against the harsh morning sunlight, he lifted his wrist to check his watch and was dismayed to see it was already 7:15 am.

"Damn" he muttered groggily, suddenly lurching into motion. He gunned the engine and tore off down the highway, quickly spotting a neon sign advertising "Mickey's Service Station" up ahead.

Twenty minutes later found Jack standing before the grimy restroom mirror at Mickey's, splashing cold water over his haggard face and scrubbing away the night's indignities with a rough paper towel. As he peered at his reflection, he traced the deep creases etched into his careworn features, seeming to study them for the first time. An indecipherable look flickered in his reddened eyes before he finished toweling off and changed into a fresh set of clothes from his duffel bag.

Back on the open road, the rumpled detective retreated within himself, sifting through the avalanche of revelations that had been uncovered over the past several mind-bending days. Fragmented scenes and snatches of dialogue flickered through his psyche like fever dreams...

Father Diaz's gentle voice echoed: "But this world works in many strange ways. Some cannot truly be explained..."

Overlaid with Margaret's imploring: "You'll have to do all you can..."

Then Kathy's soothing reassurance: "It's never too late..."

Quick cutting to Henry warning: "Things don't always appear as they really are..."

Followed by Father Diaz's beatific smile: "Well, faith is my business..."

And John Smith's probing challenge: "Mr. Peterson, if you lost your faith, well you wouldn't be praying now then, would you?"

The disjointed vignettes piled one atop the other in Jack's overwrought consciousness:

Kathy marveling, "It was...it was like she saw an angel..."

His own gruff baritone uttering a single, portentous word: "Salvation..."

Until finally, Father Diaz's kindly voice rung out clearly, as if projecting across the vast expanse of the California desert: "You know what they say, it lies within..."

Then Smith's enigmatic declaration, "It's something you've searched for most of your life..."

Eyes locked on the highway ahead, Jack felt a sudden clarity beginning to crystallize within him, an inexorable pull he could no longer resist. He knew exactly where he needed to go.

As the sun sat low over the Mojave Desert, Jack pulled up behind Kathy Burns restaurant, his gaze immediately falling on the dilapidated sailboat rotting away in the desert. He got out and slowly approached the weathered, sun-bleached hull, reaching down to grasp the bottom rung of the makeshift ladder and hoist himself up. Carefully making his way around to the stern, he paused before slowly peeling back the tarpaulin, exposing the faded lettering on the transom:

SALVATION

With a trembling hand, Jack released the canvas covering and it sloughed back into place with a muffled thump. He stood motionless for a long moment, the word seeming to reverberate in his soul. Drawing a deep, steadying breath, Jack turned and walked nimbly onto the deck. He walked around the cabin and open the hatch. He then descended into the musty interior.

His penlight cut through the gloom to reveal a sparse but relatively intact living space below decks roomy enough for modest cruises, but clearly showing its age and lack of upkeep. As his probing beam swept over the spartan furnishings, Jack noticed something out of place on the small table. An ordinary white envelope, blank but for the word "Salvation" scrawled hastily across it.

Jack moved over and sank heavily onto the cushioned bench, picking up the innocuous envelope and holding it gingerly, almost reverentially. After staring at it for an endless moment, he tugged open the sealed flap and slowly pulled out the single sheet of paper and unfolded it.

At first his eyes couldn't quite process the meaning of the simple sequence of numbers plainly handwritten on the paper:

3 - 15 - 31 - 19 - 41 - 12

Then, as the implication sank in, his features contorted in a rictus of equal parts elation and reflective sorrow. Jack carefully refolded the paper and slid it back into the envelope with a slow exhale, setting it carefully aside as he rose and made his way back up onto the deck and down the ladder.

Just then, Kathy's soft voice called out from the deepening twilight. "I knew you would do it."

Jack spun at the sound, torn from his contemplation to find Kathy smiling at him tenderly from a few feet away. Regaining his composure, he held up the envelope questioningly. "You knew about this?"

"No, not exactly," Kathy replied gently, shaking her head. "But I had a hunch, because momma was so happy when this showed up. Before she died, she said 'Don't you ever sell that boat, promise me.' And I promised." Her smile widened as she added simply, "After all this, now I know why she felt that way."

Jack looked down at the weathered watch on his wrist, the second hand sweeping on inexorably. "As they say, it's time to fish or cut bait I guess?" He met Kathy's gaze, inhaling deeply. "I suppose I've got a decision to make."

Kathy just smiled serenely in return. "Yes...you certainly do."

With a nod of finality, Jack extended his hand. "I don't understand it all yet, but thank you."

Kathy accepted the handshake warmly. "The pleasure was all mine. You take care, Jack."

He held her eyes for a long beat before turning to go.

But as he started to walk away, a thought occurred to Jack and he paused, looking back over his shoulder and turned. "Maybe you haven't seen the last of me."

A twinkle shone in Kathy's warm gaze. "Is that a promise?"

Meeting her steady regard, Jack felt his face settling into the first genuine smile in longer than he could remember. "Yes," he stated with conviction. "I think it is..."

<u>Chapter Eight</u>

~ Salvation ~

Hours later found Jack standing on the doorstep of a very small nondescript Los Angeles bungalow, his heart thundering in his chest and palms slick with nervous sweat. He glanced down at his watch once again 9:30 PM, then back up at the darkened windows, psyching himself up for what was to come. Finally, after an endless moment, he reached out and rapped his knuckles against the wooden door, his future hanging in the balance.

A moment later, the door swung open to reveal a man in his late 20s, his expression one of mild surprise to find a visitor at this late hour. But when he realized who it was, Shawn's face registered shock and something deeper, something more akin to reproach.

"Hey Dad, what's going on?" he said cautiously, as if already bracing for the worst.

But before Shawn could say anything more, Jack closed the distance in two long strides and enveloped his son in a fierce embrace, his body shuddering with silent sobs of overwhelming love, regret and unbearable hope.

Shawn stood there numbly for a long beat, frozen with confusion and disbelief. But eventually his arms came up reflexively to return the hug, his fingers digging almost painfully into Jack's shoulder blades as buried emotions welled up from some unfathomable depth.

After what could have been an eternity or just a few fleeting seconds, Jack pulled back and cupped his son's face in his trembling hands, drinking in every detail as if seeing him for the first time.

"Good to see you, son," he rasped, voice thick with unshed tears. "I've really missed you."

Still disoriented, Shawn finally managed a halting reply. "What's going on, is something wrong?"

His father was already shaking his head vehemently, an undeniable fire burning in his eyes.

"No... everything is finally right."

Jack watched his son intently as they sat across from each other at Shawn's kitchen table. So much remained unspoken between them after all these years, but Jack knew this was his chance to finally lay it all out in the open.

"I think it's time we talked," he said solemnly. "Let's go inside."

What followed was an agonizing, emotionally raw conversation that dredged up decades of resentment, anger and misunderstandings on both sides. The two men poured out their souls, shouting and weeping in equal measure as years of pent-up frustrations came spilling forth in a torrent of bitter reproaches and desperate pleas for understanding.

At one point, Shawn got up and moved around the table to console his distraught father, embracing him tightly as Jack broke down in racking sobs of regret and shame. The healing process was excruciatingly painful, like lancing a deep, long-festering wound, but it was necessary to finally clean out the emotional poison.

After what seemed like an eternity, the two sat in heavy silence, emotionally spent but feeling as though a great weight had finally been lifted from their shoulders. Jack studied his son's face, lined with the same world weariness he knew was etched into his own features. But there was also a glimmer of hope there, a hard-won peace that came with such brutal honesty.

"Are we going to be alright now?" Jack asked cautiously, hardly daring to breathe.

Shawn met his father's eyes steadily before a slow smile spread across his face, washing away years of bitterness and judgment in that one simple expression. "Yeah dad...I think so."

Jack felt his own lips curl in a tremulous smile of relief. This was the new beginning he had been seeking, the emotional redemption that had driven him on his strange journey back into his own soul. Knowing that he now had the potential to right was thought to be utterly impossible.

"If it's okay, I need to make a phone call really quick," Jack said.

"Sure, go ahead" Shawn replied easily.

As Jack takes out his cell and begin dialing, Shawn walked by his father. Jack gestured him to pause and without a word, he handed Shawn the lottery ticket from his pocket, with a nod signaling that he might want to check it. Jack released it almost reverentially as Shawn gave him a warm smile and approving nod before heading into the living room to work on his computer.

Jack completed the call, his face relaxing into an expression of contented bliss as he listened to the voice on the other end of the line.

"Hello"

"It's Jack."

"I'm glad you called, where are you?" Kathy asked.

"I'm at my son's house, we've been talking," Jack replied, his gruff voice thick with emotion. "We had a real good talk."

Unaware of the night's events, Kathy continued pleasantly, "That's great to hear. I can hear a difference in your voice. I see it's almost 11:00 now."

"I hope it's not too late. I just decided to come here," Jack said simply.

In the other room, Shawn is on the computer and suddenly exclaimed, "Dad, you need to get in here quick!"

"No. It's not too late. Ah…do you have to go?" Kathy asked apologetically.

"I got a minute..." Jack said, throwing a bemused glance toward the living room. "I'm still feeling a little strange."

"I guess that's to be expected..." Kathy said sympathetically.

Then Shawn's voice rang out again, this time with awe and elation: "Oh my God, you won! You hit it; I can't believe it!"

A knowing smile crept across Kathy's face, "It sounds like you made a stop on your way."

Jack seemed to pick up on her meaning. "Let's just say the curiosity got the best of me."

"Dad, get off that phone and get in here!" Shawn called insistently.

Laughing quietly, Kathy said, "I'll let you go, Jack. I think you've got a lot more to talk about."

"Okay," Jack agreed. "But how about lunch sometime?"

"I'd really like that," Kathy said warmly.

"Dad!" Shawn's voice demanded.

Chuckling, Jack promised, "I'd better go, I'll call you later."

"Okay, bye now."

"What did you say, Shawn?" Jack asked as he joined his son in the living room, eyes twinkling merrily. "I won? Get out of here..."

One year later…

The skies over Calgary Cemetery opened up in a torrent of cold rain as mourners gathered under a large tent for a funeral. Jack and Kathy exited the limousine, the former shielding them both with a black umbrella as they made their way up the muddy hillside toward the gravesite.

Father Diaz fell into step beside them, placing a comforting hand on Jack's shoulder. "Jack, how are you?"

"Well, as can be expected," Jack replied solemnly, his voice catching slightly.

Offering Kathy a warm if sorrowful smile, the priest said, "Very nice to see you. I wish it was under better circumstances."

"Nice to see you too, Father," she murmured, returning the sentiment.

As they neared the casket, Father Diaz inquired gently, "When we get there, would you like to say anything?"

Steeling himself, Jack gave a solemn nod. "Yes, if that's alright."

The priest assured him it would be. "of course…"

"Yes, thank you."

Jack felt a lump form in his throat as he moved to stand beside the polished casket amid the crowd of mourners, some of whom he recognized like Henry and Bell Riddell.

Others were complete strangers, brought together by the extraordinary impact John Smith had on each of their lives. He cleared his throat hesitantly and began his eulogy.

"I know many of us here were touched in one way or another by him..."

Jack's gaze fell on Kathy, her face a mask of tranquil sadness. "He always had nothing but a kind word and the best intentions for everyone he met."

His eyes lifted to meet those of each person solemnly arrayed before him. "We grew very close over this last year. But I know almost everyone here feels like we lost a very good person. You will be missed by more than the few that stand here today. You will be missed by many who never even met you." Jack swallowed hard, blinking back tears as his voice dropped to a gravelly whisper. "I am so glad that we got to know one another in the end. Now you can sleep..."

Jack stepped back and allowed Father Diaz to come forward and deliver his solemn blessing over the departed soul. As his voice washed over the mournful gathering.

Later that evening, a private wake was held at Kathy's diner, the door adorned with a hand lettered "Closed for Private Party" sign.

Outside among the many cars at the diner is a 1968 black Camaro with a black convertible top. The custom license plate is JC1968; obviously in tribute to his dear friend.

Inside, Jack sat at a table with Kathy and Father Diaz, surrounded by the other mourners milling about and reminiscing in hushed tones.

Lost in his own contemplations, Jack was pulled back to the present by a familiar voice. "How is everyone?"

He looked up to see Ben Klein, the lawyer who had first set him on this life-altering path, standing beside the table with a warm but somber expression.

"Ben," Jack exclaimed, rising to his feet and grasping the other man's hand firmly. "Nice to see you."

"Sorry I couldn't make it earlier," Ben said contritely.

Jack scoffed. "No, thanks for coming."

"If you got a minute, I need to talk to you," Ben said, pausing to glance around at the others. "If I'm not interrupting anything?"

Jack gestured for him to continue. "Sure, will you excuse us for a moment?"

Murmurs of "Go ahead" and "That's fine" came from Kathy and Father Diaz as Jack led Ben outside to the quiet lot behind the diner. They settled onto a couple of metal chairs.

"Well, it's been a crazy year, hasn't it?" the lawyer remarked.

Jack could only nod soberly. "You can say that again."

"Just to let you know," Ben said, "I didn't know anything until after."

Furrowing his brow, Jack sought clarification. "So, you know the whole thing now?"

"Pretty much, I kind of had to..."

That piqued Jack's curiosity. "Why's that?"

Ben extracted a plain envelope from his inner pocket. "I have this letter for you..."

He paused contemplatively before continuing, "It's from John. He had me draw up some documents about 6 months back and he asked me if I could give this to you...if, you know." Another weighty pause as he sought the right words. "He knew about it for a long time, Jack. It must have been...oh, a couple years I guess. That's at least what he told me."

Jack accepted the proffered envelope, holding it almost reverentially as tears stung his eyes. "Another envelope from Mr. Smith..." he murmured, sniffling audibly.

Sensing Jack needed a moment, Ben rose from his chair. "I'll let you read it alone, alright?"

His friend could only nod, already distracted by the letter in his hands as Ben headed back inside. Jack stared at it contemplatively for a long beat before slowly opening it, dabbing at his eyes with his handkerchief as he gently extracted the neatly folded stationery. Sliding on his glasses, he began to read, his lips moving silently along with John Smith's distinctive voice echoing in his mind:

"Jack, I hope this letter finds you in good spirits even if it comes on a somewhat solemn occasion. If you're reading this it means I have passed from this world and started my next adventure. I hope you realize I couldn't say anything, it was just too hard. In the time I have known you, I have come to realize that you are a very dedicated man, a dear friend and one who will keep his word.

The promise I mentioned is the one you told me about in my office that day...how you wanted to make something out of your life and that is what I am here to offer you.

This work needs to be carried on and I believe you are the man to do it. I must say something I never told you, those prayers did not come from you in the night when I first heard them, they came from others. They were the ones whose voices I heard; they were the ones who sent me to you. James and Margaret send you their love and say, 'They are very proud of you.' I wanted you to know that it was they who knew you so well and they were the ones who heard your prayers."

Jack felt tears streaming down his face as he absorbed those words, hastily wiping them away with his handkerchief as Smith's voice echoed on in his mind:

"Inside the boat is the key to the office and all the legal documents you'll need to take over the business. I know you'll know what to do, you understand what needs to be done. Salvation is not a status we achieve, it's a place where we find out why we are here...and that is our salvation. It saves us from wandering about in this world and keeps our souls content in the next. I know you will find it; I have the utmost faith in you. Good luck with everything and take care. Your dear friend, always...John."

A heavy silence descended over the deserted alleyway, broken only by Jack's ragged breaths and the discordant droning of a light buzzing fitfully above him. After an interminable moment, his son Shawn's voice called out from the street.

"Dad? You okay?"

Jack lifted his gaze, fresh tears glistening on his cheeks, to see the dilapidated form of the old sailboat the one that had set him off on this incredible, life changing odyssey, resting aimlessly in the dirt nearby. He stared at it for a long inscrutable beat before replying in a hushed tone thick with emotion:

"Sure, Son...I'm fine. I'll be right there."

And after a lifetimes journey and decades of internal suffering, at last, Jack Peterson had finally found his salvation.

The End